I0824425

The Atonement Of Nikolai Isayev

GERARDO CANOVA

ISBN: 978-9962-13-218-9

Book design and Jacket design: Gerardo Canova

First Edition

Peace and joy await for those who atone.

ACKNOWLEDGMENTS

I would like to thank my family and friends to whom my dream of becoming a writer may have never seen the light.

Thank you!

PROLOGUE

Secluded in her room, Beatrice could only imagine Nikolai laughing, playing and smiling alongside Krysi and Josephine, as the happy family he always desired to have, as they both enjoy the new revolting parenthood they have. Indeed, Nikolai had many things now to be happy, and Beatrice's grim life wasn't part of that.

Lurking in Nikolai father's room, Beatrice found a beam of light, she didn't know she would ever need; but holding the small glass bottle of opium tincture, she could only thank Natasha for her unscrupulous ways of getting rid of Nikolai's mother. And with the same idea, of using the tincture in her favour, she took a tight grip around the bottle and slowly walked away. Finding reasons to approach Josephine, when she had been rude and offensive towards her, has proven to be hard, but she wasn't going to cave in.

Two days later she found that opportunity when they both stumble front to front in one of the many corridors of the house. Josephine's reaction was to lower her head at Beatrice's striking poise.

"Josephine, I am glad I get to talk to you alone." She said looking up and down at her, and then she grabbed her hand. "Can we talk? In private."

Josephine nodded. Then Beatrice pulled her near her.

"I want you to forgive me." Her voice breaks down.

"Forgive you? Why?" Josephine mumbled.

"Oh sweet Jo…" she couldn't believe the words that were coming from her, trying not to gag, but she needed to gain her trust. "I've been so harsh on you. You really love him, don't you?"

"I – yeah I do – but…" Jo stutter.

"But what?"

"It's little awkward talking about this with you." She gave a step back.

If Beatrice wanted her to trust her she would have to open herself a little more warmly. "I know what you mean, but I'm not judging you. To be honest I have done a lot of things that can be considered bad."

"Still..." she gave another step back away, but Beatrice held her hand.

"Wait!" said with a tight grip of Josephine's hand.

"You can trust me. Think of it as a band-aid, the faster you peel it away the less painful."

"It's ok. Actually, I understand you perfectly."

"I want to get closer to you, become friends, all for Nikolai's sake. So please trust me." Beatrice pleads one last time. Inside she was furious of how much she has to lower herself to get closer to Josephine, but if she succeeded; she will no longer have to deal with her anymore.

"Well…I do love Nikolai…but I can't help myself to think about

Ivan. I know he is lost and all, and probably he might be dead now, but still. It is not easy to cope with the lying, the betrayal and not feel remorse at all." Josephine said with watery eyes.

"Now I understand why you thought it might be awkward." She took a deep breath and then continued. "What happened between me and Ivan…was a long time ago now; Nikolai's friendship has saved me from a social debacle. I care a lot about him and I have to admit you do him good." She bit her lower lip hoping Josephine will fall for her lies.

"Thank you. Honestly, Nikolai is everything I got now…well, him and Krysi."

"Now you have me. We are friends right?"

"Yes, I guess so." Josephine smiled awkwardly. Beatrice won the battle for Jo's trust and hugged her effusively.

Later that week, as things smoothed between Beatrice and Josephine, Nikolai felt it was time for Beatrice to accompany them at least during dinner. It was the polite thing to do, and he couldn't help but feel he was the cause of her ostracizing. So, with his strong manners and firm hand, he forced her to attend dinner against her will. She didn't felt she was ready to share a room with the two of them, but what other choices she had? The sole idea of being without Nikolai was too painful. She felt her life chained to his, and she was devoted to his will, to his hand and his needs. She wanted to please him, yet she also wanted him only to herself, to her command, for her needs. The way he looked at Josephine repulsed her so much, she couldn't bear much time without saying anything, and once again the evil voice in her head told her to ask for a new hunting. Masking her human blood lust for a simple thing like a hunt was a key way of speaking for her and Nikolai, and a clumsy and naïve Josephine only could ask and speak about what she knew of common hunting.

The dinner didn't end well, and as Nikolai left the dining room with Josephine to see their precious daughter, the irritated Beatrice cooked the idea unthinkable until that dinner. Looking at the empty table as Katya and the two footmen remove the half-eaten plates belonging to Nikolai and Josephine, Beatrice smiled at her enlighten new plan, lifted her glass of red wine and stare at the crimson liquid swirling around in it. Her eyes twinkle in excitement.

Nikolai left the house very early the next morning to inspect the reconstruction of Ovsky Manor, and Beatrice thought that was her chance to get her plan rolling. She wasn't going to lose much time thinking and her hands tremble of the excitement of doing what she linger every night in her deep dreams.

"Katya!" Josephine called from the stairs down, but nobody answer.

"She is gone for the day. I gave everyone the day off." The deep tone of Beatrice's voice was eerie, and Josephine jumped surprised by the sudden approach of her friend.

"You scared me!" taking gasps.

"Sorry, I just wanted to make something special for Nikolai."

"Oh, you want the house for the two of you? I can go away if you want me to."

Poor fool, she thought. "No, actually I want you to stay. And if you need any help, I'm here don't worry."

"Oh well, same goes to you, I will be happy to help you. I am going to have a shower, you don't mind taking care of Krysi for a couple of minutes do you?"

"Of course not, it will be my pleasure." She said with a big smile across her face.

She looks sickened down at the girl in the crib and brought some tea before Josephine came out of the bathroom. She sighed. The bitch did look beautiful even without makeup or only wearing a silk bathrobe and no jewelry on. Josephine smiled at Beatrice unknowing what was all about the strange closeness from her, and sat at her white vanity table.

"I brought some tea." Holding a flower detailed cup right next to Josephine.

"Thank you." She said giving another smile at Beatrice.

"May I brush your hair?" asked like a little girl looking up to her much older sister. Wanting to please her and dreaming of becoming her.

Josephine nodded and gave her the brush.

As Beatrice brushed down the silky hair strands on Josephine's head, she could stare at them, both reflected in the mirror and couldn't help but compare herself to her. The statuesque figure of Josephine against her frail self, the similar hair colors, yet hers was more washed out, due to the fact that it wasn't her real hair colour as she tried to mimic Josephine's golden locks. And how beautifully the green eyes from Josephine pop out, bright and wide, while her grey ones seem dull and lacking life.

One sip. Two sips, from Beatrice's tea.

Josephine's eyes began to fail her, and she felt she was feeling drowsy. The cup fell on the floor as she failed to put it in the right spot over the vanity table.

"Are you ok?" Beatrice's words were strange and she couldn't make out her face. Everything seems blurry.

"I am not feeling alright." She mumbled, and Beatrice smiled.

"Oh, you are." The tone of Beatrice's voice lowered, smug and malevolent.

"What have you done?" struggled to say while reaching at her with a wobbly hand in her sleepy state.

Giggling at the clumsy movements, Beatrice took Krysi in her hands and walked away from the room. Desperate Josephine didn't know what was going on, so she stood up and stumbles with baby deer-like legs until she reached the doorframe and rest her whole body against it. The blurry image of Beatrice holding Krysi and walking down the stairs terrified her. *Where is she taking her?* She thought.

"Give me back my daughter!" she screamed using almost her whole breath.

But Beatrice's laugh was all she got as a response. She took a deep breath trying to focus her sight and gave a big step out of the room. She hit the front of her hip as she leaned against the rails of the balcony and the stairs. It wasn't going to be easy, but she had to do it. Her sight was going around and around, and she wasn't sure where the first step of the stairs was. Her heart beating fast with each step she gave. When she finally reaches the bottom, she looked at the whole place moving in circles, but the giggle and laugh from Beatrice and the cries of Krysi guided her to the kitchen.

Sat in a wooden baby chair, Krysi screamed and cried uncontrollably.

"Mama is here." She said extending her arms towards Krysi, but from behind Beatrice hits her in the head with a rolling pin and she falls aching in the ground.

"You had to be so…pathetic." Beatrice crouched in front of her and lifted her head by the hair, making her whimper from the pain it caused her. "You know, I never liked you. You could have taken your whole shit and disappear, but no you have to come between me and

Nikolai." She chuckles. Her hands trembling as she stands up and gets a butcher knife from around the table in the kitchen. In her pain and exasperation, Josephine began to cry asking for Beatrice to stop, but Beatrice wasn't into listening to anyone.

"You have to stop crying!" she yelled at the baby, who scared and surprised stop her crying dry. "Look at your mama."

"Get your hands off her!" Jo manages to say in her semi-awake mind as she tried with no results to incorporate herself. She was bleeding from the wound in the back of her head.

"I am tired of you!" Beatrice said running towards her and grabbing her again by the hair and pulling it back. "I want you gone." She murmured with her lips pressed against Jo's face.

"Please don't hurt me." Pleaded while tears began to run down her cheeks. The effect of the opium tincture that Beatrice put in her tea has run off by the whole traumatic experience. "I will take my things and leave you and Nikolai alone…you won't see me or Krysi ever again… please!"

"Sweetheart," Beatrice whisper still against her cheek, "I will make sure we don't see you again." And she pressed the cold steel edge of the knife she was holding against Josephine's soft long neck. Josephine's eye widened, but immediately she closed them in expectation as Beatrice slices her throat. She stared delighted at how the flesh splits and tears, and the blood flow down on to her chest in a ruby river. She rests her back against the table's legs, while Krysi cried in the background and Josephine's body squirms until her body stops bleeding.

● ● ● ● ●

I couldn't believe what happened. I stared at my blood-spattered hands at Beatrice's deceased body next to me as I sat in the dining room floor after the violent I attack I had on her, and in the numbed state, I could vaguely listen to Krysi's cry far away. I stood up trying to keep my balance swinging over my feet and looking down at Beatrice's leaking wounded eye, I sighed and left the room dragging my feet against the wooden floor and up the stairs to Krysi's bedroom. The door squeaked as I gently pushed it open, I turn on the lights and look down on her.

"Hey, little princess!" I whispered as I leaned over her and held her with my blood stained hands.

After washing my hands I changed her diaper and packed her a suitcase. In the madness of the night, I had to keep a clear mind. I sat her in the cradle, while I quickly packed my stuff. I have to be smart, I need money if I want to go away, but anyone could trace my stuff, and I need to be untraceable. And probably when Katya came back the next day, she would call the police, and everybody would be after my daughter and me. *My daughter, in what mess I'm taking my daughter.*

I grabbed all the money I found around as fast as I could, picked krysi up and packed Josephine's remains, not before throwing my guts out completely sicken at the memory of rejoicing myself with her flesh. So with almost no planning, I drove away from the Isayev House, from my life and everything and everyone I know.

As I drove through the city, looking at all the crumbling buildings and the homeless people sitting on the sidewalks, I couldn't help but feel miserable at the huge loss I was undergoing. Though, as I pass near the hotel I remembered the safety box in father's main office, filled with money and several small velvet bags with gemstones. So before we could leave everything behind, I made a quick stop. I parked the car and look over at Krysi sleeping in the passenger seat. I bite my thumbnail and moved my legs nervously, considering all the pros and cons of going inside the hotel. I tuck krysi with a blanket carefully not to wake her up and stepped out of the car and walk towards the entrance with a fast and strong stride.

"I'm a bad father. I'm a bad father. I'm a bad father." I repeated to myself as I approach the main doors, thinking about how I unsafely left my baby daughter alone in a car, but we need the money to be able to go away. The bad action I just took its justified by the importance in a wider view.

Avoiding any direct contact with any of the employees or the guests, I walk through the lobby to the elevator and into the office. Nervously I put in the code of the vault and there it was, my little fortune; the little fortune that will help me go away with my girl and forget everything. I began putting some of the money into my pockets and grabbed a suitcase father had at the bottom drawer of his desk and throw its contents on the floor. Pens, papers, and cardholders hit the floor, and I start throwing in the small velvet bags, but suddenly the door opens behind and it startles me.

"Sir!" Denikin said also startled at my presence.

"Denikin, I didn't expect you to be this late," I answered to him.

"Yes, Sir. I just had some paperwork to do."

"Good." Looking up and down at him and back to the save and to the suitcase.

"Are you ok, Sir?" he asked with his confused expression at my strange behaviour.

"Yes!" I answered and put in the suitcase the last things in the vault, immediately closing it and walking fast pass him, avoiding any other question from his part. He stood still startled, not really knowing what was going on.

Back on the car, I checked on Krysi completely worried and

ashamed for leaving her all alone in the car. This was going to be the first and last dangerous thing I would ever put my daughter in. From now on, I will devote myself to making her safe and happy, at any costs. I start the car and drove myself away from the rotten life I had. I will start a new life, for me, but mostly for Krysi. Thankfully she won't be able to remember anything and being away, no one would ever tell her anything about the things I've done.

The soothing warmth from the morning sun hit my face gently, and I opened my eyes after a long night sleep. The soft cotton white bed sheet against my body felt really nice, and I began to remember my old bed, my silk bedsheets and the calming scent from freshly brewed coffee. The gentle touch from Katya's hand waking me up and how blessed I felt for my little life.

I stood up and walked towards the window and I could look down at the garden and at the red terracotta rooftops of my neighbour's homes. I rarely stared at the beautiful scenery of this country. It's so much different to the cold wintery scenery of my homeland Russia. I still can remember how we got here. How hard it was for me to find a sailing ship and a captain willing to take me away with my little girl. We spend a few days in Russia, while I figure out what to do and how to leave the country with her, while at the same time I could see holographic posters asking for information on my surroundings. I knew I was going to be persecuted immediately. I didn't think much about leaving everything behind, Beatrice's body, Zatara's remains and the incriminating cufflink in the freezer vault of Isayev House. I got us a small room in a cheap motel in the dangerous zones of the near town of Noginsk. It was a perfect place as no one asked any questions. The worn out, red Etruscan printed style bedsheets, the dirty wallpaper, the old T.V. set, and a frosted dirty window was all the depressing luxury I could afford now to hide. I took my shirt off and put my baby girl on the bed. My stomach turned just at the tiny thought of her skin touching those sheets. I sighed while sitting on the edge of the bed and paned my sight around. I walked to the bathroom, which looked clean overall, but the more I was in there, the more I could notice the fungus growing in the corners of the floor, a few stains on the bathtub, toilet, and sink. My saggy eyes reflected on the stained and broken mirror. I pulled my hair back and stare at my face, thinking carefully on how to change my style in order to avoid being recognized by anyone. My beard was beginning to come through as slight stubble, and as I grab my razor in my hands and was about to shave it, the idea of shaving my hair went through my mind. I ran to the room and search in my bag for my pocketknife and back into the bathroom, I began to cut chunks of hair randomly from my head. And since I couldn't afford to be on the streets buying for shaving cream, I squirt a little shampoo on my hands and began massaging my scalp until foam formed. Grabbed my razor and began shaving the rest of my hair. The warm water makes the small bathroom look like a steam room and when I was done, I gently clean the mirror with a towel and stare at my new hairstyle. I didn't look that different but at least was something that would help me get away for a few days. Tired, I fell asleep; only Krysi's crying woke me up.

I clean her, change her into clean clothes and we walked out of the motel. Gloomy, the town was already awake in its common death state; it fell into this dark ambiance after addicts and drunks took the town for their own. It wasn't a safe place, but like every town and city in the world, it had certain safer sites with good and loyal people. I found a little café, where I could have breakfast and get some mashed fruit and milk for Krysi. I sighed, saddened for the troublesome life I was upbringing my precious daughter.

"You have some proper gentleman's manners." A young woman said as she cleans a nearby table. The café was empty, but for an elderly man, my daughter and me.

"Excuse me?" I asked confused as she took me by surprise.

"And you sound like one also." She giggled. It was quite some time since I saw someone smiled, not counting my little girl. The last person I saw was Josephine; *My beloved Josephine; My poor beloved Josephine. How cruel her faith was.*

"Yah, moms teach well. Mine wanted me to become a gentleman, so I picked up a few things." I said trying to create a convincing new character.

"I think it's charming." She winked at me. "Is your wife coming by?" she asked.

"I am not married."

"But you have a daughter." Moving her eyes back and forth from Krysi sitting next to me.

"I do." I looked down. "I am a widower."

"Oh, I am so sorry." She sighed as she puts her hand over mine. A sparked went through me. It was the first human touch I had in a long time.

Without thinking it twice, neither expecting anything, she managed to get her waiter friend to look after Krysi, while she kissed me passionately in the back alley of the café. Her lips were soft, plumped and sweet. Her hands grabbed me and her nails scratched my arms, while I buried my face in her neck, as my tongue tasting her skin, my hands squeezing her round shapes strongly, almost hurting her. She moaned. She whined with pleasure.

"I don't know your name." she moaned with ecstasy as I unlaced her bodice and let her breasts feel the cold air of the morning.

"My name is irrelevant." I said, "Don't you like what are you feeling?" right before sucking and biting her left nipple.

"I do!" she screamed biting her lips, "I do!" she said again. "Take me!" she whimpered, as she untied my pants and they fell to my feet.

I lift her skirt and exhaled heavily as I entered her warmth. My eyes turned and close, as I remembered that first night with Josephine. The snow falling, the flickering fire in the background and the taste of her tongue. The girl quickly reached climax while I silenced her screaming pleasure moans and I reached mine a minute later as I remembered Josephine's emerald eyes and the touch of her hands along my body.

We walked back into the café, with little sweat on our foreheads, the girl arranging her skirt and flipping her cleaning tablecloth. I left the money for the food over the counter, picked Krysi in my arms and walked out without saying anything. I decided we needed to travel soon, so I walked towards the train station and what I saw was surprising. Holographic flyers with my face covered the columns and police officers stood all around the building, checking every man they thought look just like me. I stare at the site, biting a toothpick in my mouth, thinking what my next move should be. Krysi clung herself around my neck and I stepped back and walk away. Back the cheap motel, I couldn't help but feel upset with the whole situation and desperate on trying to keep Krysi safe.

"Housekeeping." A woman said with a gentle knock on the door.

"A moment please!" I snorted and wipe the few tears from my anger and my runny nose. I opened the door to see a thin girl leaning against a trolley with the towels, clean bed sheets, paper towels, soaps, and shampoos. The brown skirt look worn out, the cream shirt had some stains on it, her dark hair looked disheveled and her blue eyes shone from behind the tiredness of her face.

She walked in and took a look around. "I'll start with the bed." She said.

"Sure, go ahead!" I waved my hand in the air and picked Krysi in my arms.

"She seems like a quiet girl." Said while taking the used bed sheets off and extending the clean ones. After a long silence, she talked to me again. "You looked better with hair on your head." Looking up at my head and gesturing at it.

"Huh! Thanks." I rubbed my bald head and blushed a little. "I thought on getting a change, that's all."

"Well, it's certainly different." Taking the used sheets out of the room. "Soaps? Shampoo? Shaving cream?" said showing me the small bottles from the trolley.

"Yes, please!"

"The change makes you look older." Finally said before leaving.

"Oh hey!" I called her out as she pushes the trolley a little. "What's your name?"

"Aryana. Why?"

"Well…you see, I was wondering if you could look after my

daughter for a couple of hours tonight," I said and looked at how she squinted her eyes doubting me. "I am willing to pay you, I need a babysitter."

After a few seconds of consideration she agreed, and later that night, I left krysi at the front desk with Aryana. I stared down at her little brown eyes with green undertones and inhaled the youthful hope emanating from them. I wouldn't be back until I found a way for us to go away. As soon as I stepped out, the chilly wind hit me with force and I squint. I pulled the dark beanie on my head covering a little more my ears, and hugging myself I walked away from the motel.

I look around, between the dirty damped streets. The town looks emptier than in the morning, but I could see some flickering lights from a couple of bars and brothels open. I walked near one and before I went in, I look inside through the stained window, and as the same time staring at how my reflection has changed with a little beard and the baldness of my head. I walked in, and strong stench punched my senses mixed with the slight warmth from the chimney and several yellowish light bulbs, scattered around the bar in antique lamps. Nobody cared for my presence. Everyone was busy with his or her own stuff, drinking, playing cards, laughing while having scantily dressed prostitutes, enjoying their joyful time with clients. I sat on a very old stool and asked the barman for a vodka shot.

"You are not from around here." He said with his deep voice while serving me.

I stare at him. At his chubby complexion, his wrinkled and experience face, with a greyish beard and his grey eyes, under thick and bushy eyebrows. "No, I am traveling through," I said drinking my shot and asking him for another one.

"Well, this town might not seem like much, but we don't like strangers messing around." Said as he served the shot and left the bottle next to it.

"I am not looking for trouble."

"And what are you looking for?" he leaned on the top of the bar resting his forearms on it and looking directly into my eyes.

Before I could answer, a few policemen entered the bar and everyone kept silent looking at them. I gave a quick glance and crouched my head into my shoulders, praying not to be seen.

"What can we do for you gentlemen!?" The barman said walking away from me and greeting the men in their grey uniforms.

"Just a couple of beers." One of them said as they sat at a nearby table, opening their jackets and relaxing as they sit.

They got served by one of the waitresses and the whole bar slowly went back to the same atmosphere it had before their arrival.

"Try not to look suspicious." The barman muttered as he leaned in front of me.

"What?"

"I've seen a lot of stuff, and I certainly know you are trying to hide your presence from them."

"Hum! Let's say I am not in good relations with the law."

"Aren't we all?" he smirked. "So tell me, what you are looking for?"

I scratch my head and face away from the policemen. "A way to travel out of this town and maybe be able to get to a port."

"That's tricky." He said moving his head and scratching his beard. "But not impossible. Though it will cost you."

"I don't care how much it costs."

"Come back in three days, and I might have a solution to your predicament."

"Really?" my eyes widened in excitement.

"I don't promise anything kid, just come back in three days and we will see what I've got."

I cheered silently and drank to my good fortune. When I left the bar, I wasn't even paying any attention to the policemen and they were certainly not paying attention to anyone but to the four beautiful girls flirting with them. I lit a cigarette and start my journey back to the motel; I stumble upon a drunken man walking down the empty streets. The cold wintery scene and the vulnerable man reminded me of the many hunts I used to enjoy, the soft flesh being sliced apart, and the warmth of the blood spattering against my hands, my face and my body. Everything happening in any solitary alley, forest or in the shadows; the darkness was all for me, but now that Krysi was the first thing in my mind; I miss my old devious self. As I thought about all of those things, I didn't realize that I had taken the drunken man to an empty site and stabbed him several times with my pocketknife, and I stare at the dead body, licking the blood off my hands. "Not again," I told myself, as I remember my struggle to overcome the strange memory loss I used to have.

I pulled the body behind a couple of construction materials and hid it from any sight. I can't call anyone's attention. Thankfully on my black clothes, the blood wasn't visible, so when I walked in the motel and Aryana saw me while Krysi sleep on a chair next to her, she wouldn't have ever guessed what I had just done.

"You had a good time?" she asked while I pay her for the babysitting.

"I think so."

"You are not sure? She must have been lousy in bed then." Putting away the money.

"I wasn't looking for prostitutes."

"Oh, then guess you are not like other men." She said grabbing the cigarette from my mouth and smoking a little.

"Keep it!" I smiled and grabbed Krysi in my arms and went back to our room. She stayed there at the front desk smirking back at me as I walked up the stairs.

Even though I could see my reflection over and over, I still could see Nikolai behind does dark eyes, behind the beginning to bush out beard and the deprived of sleep face. So I pace in my room constantly thinking about what to do. Every time I was out with krysi, I could see the policemen with their face scanners looking out for me. The bluish hologram flyers with my face were installed everywhere. At least I wasn't a huge thing on the news, but the war with the Amerikan Empire was beginning to boil internationally. *I wonder if Sofy was fine constantly.* Armies were coming and going from countries, cities, and towns, leaving death and chaos behind them. Despair is a common denominator lately worldwide.

I left Krysi with Aryana again and walked to a nearby solitary forest with a bottle of whiskey in my hands. I stare down at the dying grass, the dry-out trees in the sterile stillness of the forest. I took a sip from the whiskey straight from the bottle and dried my lips with the back of my hand. I leaned against a huge boulder resting over the dry soil and touching the hardness of the rock I thought on maybe running against it, hitting my face against it and I stepped back looking at it. I sip again from my whiskey, building up the courage to do it. But even though all the things I've done, I couldn't just run to that boulder and hurt myself. Slightly drunk I walk back to the town already night-time and went into one of the many brothels for more booze to consume.

I didn't know how I got back into the motel room lying on my bed; all I know was that it felt good. So good I was about to burst. Warmth and wetness, sometimes, soft lips against my skin. Maybe it was a dream, a nice dream I didn't want to wake up from. It was so real I couldn't contain myself. The next day I woke up with my clothes undone, naked over the bed, with a hell of a hangover.

Detective Sawyer instincts were right. He knew from the moment hc talked to Nikolai, that he was at least the one behind the disappearance of Zatara Lukowskaia. At his desk, he had all the photos taken from the scene in Isayev House. He thought he would be able to catch Nikolai, but something must have happened. Sliding the photos and staring at them, he could remember the gruesome discovery. Isayev House, seemed eerily silent when they arrived, and he called at the door opening it slightly, creaking from the hinges. Their steps echoed in the emptiness of the house as they walked in, a strange smell came through, no lights on and an eerie sensation of solitude.

"Be careful." He warned everyone as he takes his white gun in his hands.

"Your Excellency?" he called out and his voice travelled through the whole house, bouncing the walls and the columns, but nobody answers. He could sense the emptiness weighing on his shoulders as his footsteps creaked on the wooden floor. He walked to the living room and saw nothing but the slowly dying fire.

He swallowed thick saliva as he pushes the door leading to the dining room, and as he walked in, he notices a shiny pair of heels covered in crystals. And as far as he went, he slowly began to see Beatrice Rozanova's body lying on the floor with blue lips and snow-white skin; a bloody knife stuck to one of her eye sockets and dark spots around her neck. He looked away disgusted with the finding. The table was set in an elegant feast, as if all happened during a peaceful moment during the evening. Still, the plates had some food, and the beef was still set aside waiting to be carved and eaten. He walked into the kitchen and his eyes widened in shock, while his jaw dropped. The floor, the stove, the counters, and even the ceiling were stained in blood. It was a blood bath. The policemen couldn't resist the nauseating scene, and they ran out of the house to throw up whatever they had in their poor stomachs. Detective Sawyer was disgusted too, but he tried to keep composure over all the blood, the filth, and the pestilence.

"Call the forensics." Sawyer ordered to the policemen, who were recovering outside the house.

Later, he saw how the forensics took photographs, measure everything and packed everything they consider as evidence. The investigation at Isayev House took several days; during the ones, they found the macabre truth regarding Zatara Lukowskaia's whereabouts. His heart broke down into pieces when he had to tell her tragic fate to her parents Olga and Dmitri Lukowsky. Watching someone suffer was the hardest thing about his job, and he couldn't believe the times he had Nikolai right in front of him. If only he knew sooner. With their hands covering their faces and holding onto each other, Zatara's parents sobbed in the interview room of the police department. He left them to console each other after their loss, walking out of the room and standing alone on the hallway.

"Sir?" Theresa Yerokhin, a collegue, called him as she walked towards him.

"Hey!" he sighed looking down, his defeated expression said it all.

"You just told them, huh?" she said looking at the sobbing parents through the small window of the interview room.

"I didn't get in the force for this. I want to prevent everyone's suffering." His voice broke as he spoke. "I want to catch the criminals, the bad guys."

"I know." She gently put her hand on his arm giving him some consolation. "And you will."

"I'm doubting that…" he said but immediately paused, "You know? I had him in my hands and I let him go away."

"No, you didn't. Unfortunately, he was a Minister and you couldn't go arresting people without the right evidence in your hands." She said stepping in front of him and grabbing his face with her two small hands. He stared into the deepness of her baby blue eyes, and for the first time in his fifteen years of working in the force and five working with her, he notices her delicate features, her big eyes, her thin nose, and her small, rosy lips.

After the whole thing with Zatara's parents, the police had to take action into finding Nikolai. It was clear he ran away, and before he could go further away, they had to do something. So they send out their teams to put up holographic flyers all over the city with Nikolai's face, send a press release and go back to Isayev House and the Ministry to find out where he could have gone to. Resources were limited, after the recent bombardment by the Amerikan's, but Vladimir wasn't going to let Nikolai go away easily. Yuliya couldn't fathom what was being told about her boss, and she tried to follow detective Sawyer as he walked in the ministry's floor, towards Nikolai's office.

As if things weren't in good terms politically with other countries and the constant dispute with the Amerikan's, the Hall of Ministers was under constant pressure. But Vladimir didn't care much about the ministry, so he asked for interviews with all the ministers by himself, and the rest of the ministry officials. Every piece of information they could get from them was gold to finding Nikolai.

"No luck finding the Duchess Voronova?" he asked taking a sip of his coffee while sitting on his desk at the police department.

"No, sir. And with the duke missing, her family recently deceased it's hard." A nearby officer said.

The whole department kept silent when the first minister of security Ator Pozharsky walked in the office. His royal blue suit, his red minister's band, and the gold embellishments and jewel medals, stand out over the dull and monochromatic environment of the department. He walked in followed by his guards, while everyone stares back at him.

"I need to talk to Detective Vladimir Sawyer." He said looking around at the whole floor.

"Here, you Excellency," Vladimir said walking towards minister Pozharsky. "Let's talk in the interviewing room, follow me." Leading the way.

• • • • •

Rupert arrived at the Peninsula port looking refreshed from a long holiday away. They could have cut the trip short due to the war with the Amerikan empire, but Grisha's parents suggested not to risk their lives coming back while the stability of the country was so shaky. Grisha leaned against Rupert's arm as he descended the ship avoiding a fall on the deck. They both smiled at each other. Clearly, the trip was good for Rupert, whose obsession with Marci was driving him crazy.

The two friends seemed closer than ever and their chauffeurs drove them back into the city. As the carriages drove in, they stared startle at the destruction left behind by the Christmas attack. They knew it was terrible, but they had imagined it as less devastating, in fewer ruins that the reality. Grisha's eyes tear up as they watch the homeless poor people lay around on the streets starving, in their worn-out clothes and dirty faces. Kids with dirty hands eating out small portions of food been served by religious people and good Samaritans. It was too much and he had to look away.

"It's ok." Rupert gently rubbed his arm, then he glances back and thought on how things have changed. The lower class buildings weren't that outstanding before, but now, it was all ruins, and the opulence of the grandiose houses of the rich was almost gone.

Back in Rupert's house, he realized his parents had gone away while their Manor was being reconstructed. At least part of it was ready so they could stay until Grisha could travel to see how his parents were doing in the countryside.

"I wonder how Nikolai is," Grisha said throwing himself on the couch.

"We can go to Isayev House tomorrow. We need to get some rest." Rupert said extending his hand to Grisha and waiting for him to take it.

Grisha smiled, gently hold his hand tightly, and Rupert pulled him up from the couch and wrapped his other arm around Grisha's waist, keeping him tight against his body. He stared down at Grisha's twinkling eyes. He conducted him to his room. Few candles were lit, as the electricity wasn't back on yet on Belisnky Manor. Grisha sat in the comfy bed, with the silk cream coloured bedsheets while Rupert stood right in front of him. He lifts Grisha's head from the chin and slightly moving his hand over his cheek and brushing his fingers over his lips. Grisha moved his hands up to Rupert's face, right before he leaned in and kissed him passionately. Grisha trembled at the contact. With his eyes closed, he lingers for Rupert's lips back against his, when Rupert stood up and open his shirt, revealing his toned body. They then stare for a couple of seconds, before Grisha's hands traveled along Rupert's abdominals, to his chest and again to his face. He studied the contours, the hardness of the muscles, and the softness of his skin. He lay on the bed and Rupert climbed over him, kissing his neck and listening to Grisha's moans of pleasure filling the room. The night was cold, but inside Belinsky Manor, the lovers didn't notice as they held their nudeness tight and under the soft duvets of Rupert's bed. Grisha always tried to hide his attraction, and Rupert never knew his true feelings towards Grisha until that trip that changed their lives. And as they fuse in each other's arms, they thank the goddess of fortune to giving them the opportunity to find comfort, solace, and love, in a crumbling society due to war and hate.

Grisha woke up to the scent of coffee been brewed and his eyes stared at the ceiling in Rupert's bedroom. He smiled as he remembers last night encounter with his love. He bit his lower lip and stretched his body, whining with the thought of Rupert's hands over his body, the wetness of his tongue and the tenderness of his touch.

"Good morning," Rupert whispered leaving a tray on the bed end table and sat next to him. "Do you sleep well?" he asked moving

Grisha's hair away from his forehead.

"Yes." He smiled, seeing his reflection on Rupert's greyish eyes.

Even though he didn't look like the softest of men, Grisha had found a way to bring out a caring gentleness of his personality that he hasn't really shown to anybody. And he always wondered, since the first time they inadvertently kiss while swimming at the beach, if he has always had those inner feelings towards Grisha. It wasn't like he looked for it. It was more like love found him.

After breakfast in bed, the two of them got ready to go and see Nikolai at Isayev House, but when they arrived, they saw fluorescent teal police tape across the front door and they look confused at each other.

"What you think has happened?" Grisha asked walking to the door and putting his right hand on it.

"Maybe it has to do with the attack on the city." Rupert put his hand on Grisha's shoulder and tightens his grip.

"Gentlemen!" a police officer approached them from behind. "This is a crime scene, you are not allowed to be here."

"A crime scene?" Grisha's jaw dropped.

"What happened?" Rupert asked to the officer that looked stern at them.

"I can't discuss an on-going investigation with civilians."

"Is there anyone we can talk to?" Rupert's voice slightly stuttering, "We are friends with the Isayev's. We are close with minister Nikolai Isayev."

The officer's eyebrow lifted doubting his remark but asked them to wait and he called out detective Sawyer, who told him to send them to the police station for him to interview them.

"There's something wrong," Grisha said while they were on the way to the station. Rupert's arm around him with his comforting touch, while they both shared the strange feeling of tragedy approaching them.

THREE

Waiting for the night to arrive was desperately boring. I could almost taste the freedom, but I am so tired. Anyone would wonder why I was physically tired if all I am doing is sitting around, but I am worse than physically tired. I am mentally tired. I brought this upon me. I know. I am not a good person, maybe I was one once, but not anymore. What I've done deserves no merit at all. But I am pushing through all this tiredness and disgust with myself, not for me, but for Krysi.

How different life would have been?

My eyes began to drift away as I imagine Krysi's life.

Krysi would have grown in a magnificent home, full of love, beauty, and happiness. I can listen to the music of her first ball. The big smile on her face just like her mother's, and her long and wavy blonde hair, cascading down to her waist. Her body wrapped in a beautiful dress resembling watercolour splatters over the several layers of the sheer and soft fabric of the skirt. Little crystals embroidered, shimmering as she descends the stairs and everyone gasps at her beauty; her delicate frame in its full glory when a gentleman asks her out for her first dance in society. All the girls watching, dying of jealousy; wanting to be like her or be friends with her, or simply pretending to be better than her.

But my gracious Krysi flaunts herself in the ballroom, swifts her dress in magical elegance that can only be taught by her own mother. Josephine. I could see her standing next to me with her arm around mine, smiling at our daughter; the precious jewel of the Isayev House. On the other end of the ballroom, Sofy, my beloved sister, puffs up her layered pink dress with butterfly details. And father standing proudly next to her.

Suddenly from the corner of my eye, I saw a figure walking towards us. A woman in a tight black dress with little black diamonds, shimmering as they cast the light from the lamps, and my heart stopped as I could see her more clearly; escorted by dark knights behind her. Her thin-framed under the magnificent dress effortlessly floats in the room, and her face remains hidden underneath a massive crown headpiece, also with black diamonds. Her bright grey eyes stared piercingly at me. She slowly slides the headpiece up, revealing small rosy plucky lips and a tiny nose.

I don't really know who she was, but I felt her proximity dangerous yet at the same time inviting. Suddenly all the beauty reversed, and I found myself stepping away from her, sorting myself between the crowd, as she floats near me, moving her fingers trying to grab me with her gloved thin hands. I couldn't scape her reach and as I trapped myself against a wall, I felt the coldness of the leather black gloves against the skin of my face, and she opens slightly her mouth to say something to me; but instead, streams of blood gushes out of it, showering me all over. I even tasted the flavour of the warm blood that fell inside my mouth.

I woke up startled on my chair, sweating profusely and trying to catch my breath. I look around the room and no one was there except for Krysi. I should already be used to these strange, yet realistic dreams I always seem to have. I put my hands over my face, rubbing it slightly while I stretch my back across the bed. Tonight it's the night I must go back to that bar – I thought while Krysi crawled over to me and began playing with my face, giggling and smiling.

"Daddy it's going to leave you tonight for a while." I turned over and caressed her baby cheeks with my right hands.

Leaving her in the hands of Aryana, I covered myself with my coat before going out of the motel on my way to the bar. A slight cold rain was pouring outside. Icy water pierced my cheeks like needles as I walk through the empty dark alleys of the town. The bluish tones from several holographic 'wanted' posters with my face on it, casting their light on the cobbled ground. My soles shifting and shafting against the stones with my strong stride and my breath condensed in front of me as I exhale.

I stood still across the street from the bar. Policemen were setting up a poster on the wall outside. The fluorescent light lit up a little bit the street for a couple of seconds until it dimmed down, adjusting its contrast. As soon as they walked away, I look around, reassuring myself it was safe for me to go across the street, and by covering up my lower face with my black scarf I walked towards the bar with a normal pace; not strong or fast, neither sloppy and slow. Too slow of a pace would give my presence notoriety. Too fast and I'll be pointing arrows at me like saying 'Here I am!'.

Those couple of meters were long and all I repeated myself don't mess this up! Don't mess this up! in my mind.

The heat from the inside surrounded my face as I stepped in. The gloomy atmosphere from the bar was the same as the night from a while ago. The same old sad, lonely souls, drinking their sorrows away; the same working ladies, some with their cleavages exposed or showing off their long legs, while their clients fondled them, making them laugh and giggle. I sat at a stool and rested my elbows on the top of it. After giving the respective drinks to other clients, the old barman walked towards me and asked me what I wanted. I ordered a glass of vodka and while cleaning the wooden surface of the top with a dirty cloth he suggested me for trying a special brand of vodka he has in the back, lifting his bushy white eyebrow and staring directly into my eyes. I nodded and followed him to the back. Boxes pilled and empty bottles scattered around in the darkroom were everything I could see. But once we were there, the old man pushed three stacked wood boxes, which looked really heavy but were surprisingly light, revealing a small entrance on the floor.

Going down into the darkness, I couldn't help but reminiscence Rozanov manor and the countless nights I spent in the basement under the maze; with Beatrice's wickedness wit, her icy eyes and delicate touch. I know in the end she became mad, but sometimes, I miss her old self. I miss the young, broken-hearted girl, who seek vengeance and safety with me. My dear Jo, I am really sorry for orchestrating your downfall. I wanted to hurt her, but at a certain moment, I thought it could be possible for us to work things out with Ivan out of the picture; I never thought Beatrice was going to become dangerous.

In the darkness, a slight light peeked from the small opening below a door. The hinges cried a little as the old man pushed the door open and I had to squint at the blinding brightness from the inside.

"I've got to know that my people are safe." He said looking back at me in the eye, defying me.

"What do you mean?"

"You know what I mean –" he commanded, crossing his arms around his chest. "Your face is plastered all over the town. Who knows – where else?" leaning forward, his face menacing my personal space.

"I don't know what you are talking about." I kept my face straight, trying not to sell myself.

"He won't talk –" a woman bossed out pushing a chair towards the small table, only showing under the light her hands and forearms, rings on her fingers, and tattoos growing up both arms. "You know how these renegades and criminals are."

"Who is she?" I asked tilting my head to one side.

"She is going to be your new nightmare, pretty boy." The old man said walking out and leaving me behind with the woman.

I stared at her as she walked in the light and sat on the chair, dressed in black, with her short and choppy rosy blonde hair, in defiance of social conventions, covering her left teal eye. Her caramel skin was almost covered all over with the tattoos I saw on her fists and arms. She was definitely a lady; you could notice it in her voice, her manners, yet she commanded respect with her attitude.

"I know who you are."

"No, you don't." I dragged myself and sat on the other side of the table.

"Look, you don't fool me, but you only need to fool them –" she said pointing up to the ceiling in one only sign that I could take as the police and soldiers. "My men and I are not here to judge. We offer a service and you pay. And for what I know –" lifting her eyebrows up, " you got means to pay our services."

She clearly knows about me. *I don't know why the hell I thought a simple buzz cut; a beard and lack of sleep might change my face somehow*. I might not be easily recognizable, but if they dig deeper into me anyone could recognize me.

"There are only three things you can do about your face –" she stood up and walked around the table and behind me, holding my shoulders with her hands. "1. Surgery 2. Someone to beat the hell out of you, breaking your bones, leaving you unrecognizable. 3. Hiding for so long, that people forget about you eventually." Whispering to my ear. "I wonder how much are you willing to do to go away."

I sat still, frozen in my place, my heartbeat rising thinking about her words. *How much am I willing to do?* I have done enough, perhaps that's why she asked that; perhaps she knows I am willing to do anything. *I've murdered coldly with my bare hands. I've sent my best friend to war, to steal his wife's heart. I've eaten people's flesh and rejoice myself with their blood. I love watching the last breath leaving the body as well as their souls.*

"I'm willing to do whatever it takes to go away." I said as she sat back again in front of me, "As you said money is no problem, though I have a girl with me and I don't know if that's going to be a problem for you and your men."

"A girl? Nobody said anything about children." She sounded upset and jumped up hitting the table with her fists. "I don't work with children."

"Please!" I jumped also but I kneeled before her, "I will pay you double, triple – you name it – She is my daughter, I will do anything"

She looked down on me with a strange mix of disgust and

sadness. It was like if something inside was stopping her from turning my job down.

"I knew a man like you a long time ago." She kneeled facing me. "He was my father and –" her voice broke, "If only he had the chance to save me and my family." She said.

"What happened to him?"

"He was a good man." She said avoiding the question. "I will help you, but you will do as I say."

"I said I would do whatever."

FOUR

"So you haven't heard anything from Mr. Isayev in months." The officer said while typing down the information on his computer.

"No, I haven't. Like I said I was abroad with my friend." Grisha answered glancing back at Rupert on the other desk talking to another officer.

"I was in a bad place when Marci disappeared, I didn't believe in the law and I had to go away," Rupert said resting his back on the chair.

"I don't know any of these people…" Grisha said flipping through the photos of the victims and suddenly he stopped, "Are you showing the two of us the same set of photos?" he asked staring at the photo on his hands.

"Of course we are, why?" the officer said while giving a smirk at him.

Grisha glanced back at Rupert and saw his hands trembling, his eyes wide and his jaw about to drop.

"Don't look at that!" he stood and ran to Rupert's side, pushing the photographs away in the desk. The officer ran after him and held his arm, trying to drag him off from Rupert, but Grisha wouldn't move away. In the photograph, they both saw the yellow tones of the dress Marci was wearing the night of Rupert's party, all drenched in black stains from dirt and blood, all ragged and torn apart. Rupert swallows as he controls himself. He spent a long time trying to overcome the disappearance of Marci, as he felt responsible for that.

"Please put it down," Grisha said putting his hands around Rupert's while he still held the photograph in it. His hand trembled, unable to let go; his eye filled with tears, remembering the impotence, the despair. "Please put it down." He whispered gently, pleading him to leave it.

Rupert turned to him slowly almost shaking, "I can't." he cried, asking for help, and his mouth quivering.

"Of course you can." He answered softly. Grisha's tender ways were everything he needed, everything powerful enough to tame his emotions. Gently, Grisha pushed his hands down to the desk and with care opened his stiff fingers around the photograph. "See." He smiled. "We need some time to compose ourselves." He said to the officers.

"Sure!" one officer said. "But first answer me this, why you two got disturbed by the photographs."

"You are an idiot!" Vladimir yelled as he walked in. "He is Rupert Belinsky, didn't you do homework?"

"Sir, I did. But I don't see the relation."

"Marci Weston is suspected to be one of the victims and she disappeared from his home." He said putting the photographs away. "I am sorry gentlemen, forgive the incompetence of the department."

Looking hard on the officers.

• • • • •

Still, in exile, Natasha wouldn't let anyone notice their political status, not even while not being able to leave the mansion they live in. Her purple dress kisses the floor as she paces the studio bored of the containment. She felt captive looking through the window onto the streets. Two army men stood still, none of the two move even to sneeze or to scratch, in their green uniforms at the front fence of the mansion.

"This is a prison." She muttered between her teeth, clenching them tightly.

"Dinner is ready my lady." A maid said standing by the door with her face looking down to the floor.

Natasha didn't answer. She simply turned around and walked past her towards the dining room, but not before looking down on the girl, and lifting her chin as high as she could. She wasn't used to these amerikan maids. But she had to be grateful that at least the Amerikan's gave them the privilege to have a couple of maids for their social status.

The simple dining room was as boring as the food they got served. Disgusted she forced herself to eat the coleslaw soup with pieces of carrots and potatoes, stale bread and water. Sofy didn't receive any special treatment as a child; she also had to eat the same things as her parents, and Anatoliy barely touches his meal, disappointed on not being able to get out of that situation. Only Sofy's giggling and mumbles were the hype notes of their lives there; she wasn't aware, for how young she was, of the whole political ordeal they were in.

A siren began to scream all around town, startling them in their sits. Anatoliy ran to the window as the thumping sounds of the army boots from soldiers marching in the town from down the street the mansion was.

"Something is happening." He said frowning his eyebrows.

A couple of soldiers went in the property and knock loudly on the door. Making the whole mansion tremble with the strength of the knocks. The maid answered the door and they could hear the voices of the soldiers.

"It's nothing good," Natasha said stepping next to him with Sofy on her hands.

A knock on the door made the two of them turn around and face it with a terrifying look on their faces. A woman in uniform walked in with a digital device on her hands. Her brown eyes were bright and her honey like hair was tied perfectly; Her red lips wide in a big smile, showing off her white teeth. She dragged one of the chairs from the table and sat crossing her legs and staring condescendingly at them.

Natasha gazed at the lustrous black pumps, her shimmering and silky mocha skin, the black pencil skirt, the white blouse under a black jacket; with medals dangling down from the chest and shiny black cords on her shoulders, swinging down in a loop, pinned to the chest.

"Please have a sit." She said pointing at the other chairs at the table. The two swallow saliva, not knowing the truth about her presence in their captive home. "I won't take much of your time – I am sergeant Davis –" continued while they could listen several soldiers coming in the house. "Due to certain events, we will change the terms of your stay here in our lands."

"What events? We haven't had access to communications to talk to our families or see the news." Anatoliy grunted in anger for the lack of communication they've had.

"You are right. Perhaps I owe a little history to you." She began and as their wooden drawers were ram sacked by the soldiers, looking for everything valuable. They listened to how the attack on Moscow went, how they torture the soldiers they found spying on the Amerikan government and how after all the destruction left behind, after all the citizens held political prisoners; the Russian empire wasn't interested in saving them, all these while their clothes flew in the air, the jewels packed in bags.

"I don't believe that!" Natasha said holding Sofy tightly.

"Believe whatever you want." she slides things on the screen of the device. "The truth is that we won't longer keep this home as your lodging. All Russian citizens are being moved to more modest accommodations." Glancing at the whole dining room.

"We are noble peo…" Natasha tried saying but immediately got shut by Sergeant Davis.

"You are no noble here, and right now, your lives belong to us." She said standing up, while a soldier walked in holding some clothes on his hands. She walked towards them swinging her hips, stopping in front of Natasha and she gently brushed Sofy's hair locks. "Change your outfit, you can't go out looking like that." the soldier throws the clothes over the table.

"I won't put on those rags."

"Natasha, do as the sergeant says." Anatoliy interrupted her picking up the clothes in his hands.

"Be a man! Protect your damn family!" Almost crying.

"Listen to your husband, you don't want my men to undress you." Sergeant Davis turned around and stood behind the soldiers.

"Natasha!" he yelled, calling her attention, almost ordering her to give up. She stood frozen in her place doubting whether to do as she was told or go with her guts and fight.

"Guys, please help lady Isayeva change." Sergeant Davis ordered losing her patience.

"Please, don't!" He pleaded.

The soldiers doubted, but sergeant Davis was already tired and pace faster towards Natasha and rips her dress down from her shoulders. Natasha screamed terrified. Anatoliy and the soldiers stood surprised at the sudden rage from sergeant Davis. Natasha trembled like a baby deer, and Sofy cried with all the power of her lungs.

"Now change!" she ordered yelling at her in the ear making her jump.

"We will…give us some privacy at least," Anatoliy asked reaching to Natasha and covering her bare shoulders and part of her breasts.

She agreed and she left the dining room with the soldiers. Under Sofy's intense crying, the two of them change into the grey clothes they were given. A blue stitched insignia resembling the antique order of St. Andrew contrasted on their chests. Sofy was all red, her cheeks wet from her tears, and her voice almost gone from all the crying. Natasha loses down her hair and a few tears ran down her cheeks. They stepped out and stumble with the maid and the soldiers looking at them with pity and sergeant Davis looking at them with disgust. She gave a few steps facing her prisoners and look up and down on Natasha.

"You won't need this where you are going!" ripping the amethysts necklace around Natasha's neck. She whined at the burning pain it left her.

As they were escorted out of the house, they could see other nobles and Russian citizens being treated like cattle on the streets. No distinction between the rich and the poor. To the Amerikans they were all equal. Fear filled the air outside. Desperate sobbing all around, silenced only by the voices of the Amerikan's military men and their boots marching. What was once a quiet street where they were held captive now was a bursting hell of inhuman treatment. Everyone cried equally in an unknown situation.

"I like the girl!" Sergeant Davis said as they stepped onto the street. "I'll bring her with me."

"No!" Natasha and Anatoliy cried as Sofy was taken from their arms. She waved trying to reach them, but as tiny as she was, the soldiers ripped her from her family. Anatoliy fought back trying to get his daughter but a soldier kicked him on the stomach making him surrender and gasping for air. And Natasha felt on the ground pleading for mercy, crying her lungs out. Davis didn't bother and grabbed Sofy in her arms and walked away escorted by some soldiers, disappearing in the crowd.

FIVE

As I walked back to the motel, I couldn't help but finally feel encouraged for life, and full with hopes; that I will finally be able to give Krysi an escape from my evil past. I might not be the right person to raise her, but she is all I have right now, and I know she would make me a good man. Father consorted with Natasha and I couldn't rule out his involvement in mother's murder, and Sofy; *My dearest Sofy*; she was in the middle of everything, yet she was the product out of Natasha's deceit. It's funny that after the Christmas attack we haven't received any other, but perhaps it could mean they are preparing for a new one. The Amerikan's has proven to be tough soldiers and they never give up. Shaking my head, I told myself not to think on any political stuff, as it wasn't my business anymore. I never thought I was going to end up being a fugitive. A criminal. I could see the motel on the other side of the street, the blue light of the holographic posters hitting the floor and the walls of the buildings, and I sigh relieved.

The old tiles on the floor of the lobby shone back with the blue hues of the posters as I stood at the front desk; my fingers jumped up and down nervously as I waited, expecting Aryana to come out from the back office with Krysi; but as the time passes my eyes began to wander around the room. It seemed like the lobby has been unattended for quite some time. A cup of coffee sat cold over the counter. Several papers scattered around and some mail unopened. I call out for Aryana, but only silence answered me back. Oddly, the motel seems empty no bellboy, no concierge clerks woman, no maids. I wasn't sure what was truly going on, but the silence was a little bit unsettling. My feet slide on the floor around the front desk and I stare at every object on top of it. I pushed open the small office's door slightly and my eyes caught small bloodstains on the floor. The stains grew bigger as I step further inside the office and laying dead on the desk chair, the old concierge woman with several stabs on her body. I glance down at the wounds, oozing a little blood still and I leaned forward near her face and smelled the aroma of death. My mouth watered, delighted in the scent, remembering the last contact I had with an actual prey. I exhaled heavily and walked away. Despite it being truly my utmost desire to experience once more the constant hunt and the taste of the flesh and blood, Krysi was still missing; perhaps Aryana is granting me one last hunt before we go away.

My steps echoed against the walls of the corridors. I could feel it growing, getting longer as I glanced at a maid lying on top of the trolley with a kitchen knife on her back. I pass my hand over the body, imagining the maid's life leaving her body and sensing the strength of the killer as he held the weapon.

Why would anybody do all these? I wonder, yet still, I wasn't the right person to judge anyone's motives to take someone's life, but I am beginning to sense Krysi's disappearing, had something to do with all this death around me.

I opened my room's door wide and it was in the same state I left it. No maid came into my room to make the bedsheets. I stepped in and turned around looking at every detail of my room. I opened the bathroom's door and nobody was there. I had enough of the cold search I was conducting and rage started rising. With a strong pace, I walked towards the dead maid and I pulled the knife out of the body, cleaning the blood on the sleeve of my coat and checked on the body. I could still move her limbs and her muscles were still soft to the touch. I glanced back at my room and stare at the place I left Krysi's bag and it wasn't there. My eyes filled with tears out of anger. My breath became strong with every second and the grip on the knife got tighter and tighter. *What about the rest of the guests?* I thought, squinting at the strange silence of the whole motel. I opened the door of the room across my room and gave a quick glance in. Nobody has rented that room.

I walked back to the front desk as fast as I could and checked the keys of the rooms. It seemed they have only rented very few rooms. I look up and stare at the walls, thinking about what to do and where to go. The knife rested on the top of the desk and suddenly, shifting noises came from a room behind inside the back office. Tightening the grip on the knife I picked it up and slowly walked towards the door. My eyes shimmered under the light of the lamps, I could taste the hunt; the flavour of the unexpected victim, the fear they exuded, while a cold sweat drop fell down my forehead. Someone was hiding. My left hand grabbed the cold handle of the door and slightly twisted it to the right opening the door, the hinges crying as I pulled it open. A woman beat down with her hands on her back, and cloth shutting her mouth, crouch on the corner of the pantry room. She sobbed uncontrollably when she saw me at the door, thinking it would be the perpetrator back for her head. I kneeled before her, leaving the knife down carelessly on the floor next to me, pleading her to calm herself down and telling her I would help her.

"Who did this to you?" I asked as I ripped the cloth around her mouth.

"A…Aryana!" she sobbed.

My eyes lowered. My instincts weren't so rusty after all. "Please help me." The girl squiggled on the floor.

"Did she told you where she was going?" my voice lowered angrily.

"No, she was mumbling about leaving and about what things she needed…. Please untie me."

Her eyes widened and her jaw dropped, losing almost her breath when she saw me standing up, grabbing the knife from the floor and walking away from her. She yelled asking me for help but I ignored her. Her voice faded as the door closed shut behind my back. There were only very few options to leave the town, one of those was paying someone to smuggle you out, having a car and the other one was the train which of those was highly guarded. Tapping my fingers on the front desk while having the knife resting on its top I consider every possibility. Then I realize that she needs to be fast but still needed to plan it carefully, so she couldn't be very far.

I turned around, walked back to the small room where the girl laid on the floor still tied up from her wrists. I kicked open the door making her jump and scream at the surprise. Fiercely I grabbed her by the hair on her nape and pushed her up towards me as I kneeled staring right at her.

"Where does she live?" I hissed at her as her face showed the pain I was inflicting on her.

She cried scared at the unknown.

"Tell me!" I yelled tugging her slightly from the hair.

"Down the street!" She screamed in pain. "Please don't hurt me!"

"Down the street where?" ignoring the pain, ignoring her plea.

"In the red brick building with white windows!"

I lifted her again contemplating the beauty of her expression and I throw her back again to the floor in the same quick manner I pulled her. She tried to crawl after me but the door shut at her as I walked out of the office.

Hang in there my beloved Krysi. How far are people willing to go to harm us, was everything I could think as my shoes sunk in the soft white bed of snow gathered outside on the sidewalk. The anger inside me made my body immune to the chilling temperatures outside. The whole world around me stopped. The presence of the policemen all around the town wasn't a concern anymore. I strolled down the sidewalk, passing by on walkers, and not caring for policemen noticing me. The knife's blade, hidden under my cuff, twinkle as the lights of the street lamps and inside the buildings hit me; and the melting snowflakes sparkled as glitter all over my face. My eyes look dead. Without Krysi my whole soul was gone, my whole life was meaningless.

I stood in front of the main door of the bricked wall building with white windows. The knife slides down my hand and I grabbed it by the handle. The blade shone, I brushed my fingers against the wooden door as I stare at every crevice in it, every window in the building and suddenly I clawed my nails on it with anger.

Shifting and shuffling noises from inside the building came to me. Then I knew I was right. Aryana was in there with my girl. Strangely Krysi wasn't crying or making any noise. That little thing was making me unease deep down my core. Music played rumbling through the corridors of the house. The accordions, the violins, the cellos; I close my eyes for a second in reminiscence of the old good days back at home. I look around carefully for a way in, but everything seemed tightly close, and suddenly something hit me; I doubted the door would be unlocked, yet this whole thing was so poorly executed that staring at that little brass handle gave me a little suspicion. I grabbed the cold brass, feeling the temperature transfer to my palm, giving shivers to my arm. With all the luck that could fell on me, I turned the handle to the right and it slowly began to turn.

● ● ● ● ●

Calmly, Nikolai disappeared in the obscurity of the insides of the bricked house, with the knife on his right hand and all his senses ready for whatever he would encounter. A staircase on the right appeared in front of him. He turned his head to his right and stare at an austere and dusted living room. He turned his head to the left and took a quick glimpse of the kitchen counters. More shifting noises came to his ears and with his eyes, he tried to locate the place they came from. The wooden stair steps began to cry at the whole pressure his body weight was putting on them.

Unaware of his presence, Aryana moved stuff around, pulling clothes out of drawers and packing them in raggedy bags. Krysi lay still over the flowery bedsheets. With his agile and silent movements, he opened the door slightly and stared from behind it at her frantic search. His eyes fell upon his beloved daughter lying over the bed, and his hand tightens the knife's handle. She could have avoided everything that followed. She could have even forgotten about the ludicrous plan of stealing a child from her only parent. Instead, the cards fell over her fateful destiny and there wasn't a way back.

That night imprinted on him. Feeling the waves of the ocean hit the hull's ship, Nikolai held Krysi on his lap, while staring at the cargo surrounding them and his thoughts travel back and forth from that night. Tiny glimpses of the horror in Aryana's eyes, her screams, her pleading voice when he pulled her up from her hair and then throwing her back to the floor violently; The numbing sensation of the knife's blade slicing the soft and tender flesh of the young woman, and the soothing warmth of her blood covering his hands.

He brushes Krysi's golden curls with his left hand and starts humming the same song his mother used to sing him. Resting his head against the hull, he closed his eyes, caressing his baby, relieved in the soon final escape.

"Tili Tili bom, Zakroy glaza skoree, kto-to hodit za oknom I stuchitsya v dveri…Tili Tili bom, krichit nochnaya ptitsa, on ezhe probralsya v dom k tem, komu ne spitsya…On idet,…On uzhe…Blisko." Natasha hummed crouched in the corner of the cold barracks she was imprisoned, looking through the little crevices of the wood pallet walls at the rainfall making puddles in the mud. She pulls down the stale, grey and raggedy dress the soldiers gave her to wear, trying to hide her bare feet. Her hands slowly covered her face in desperation and then she grabbed her buzz cut head. Her long wavy brown hair was gone. Her fingertips brushed the small hairs left on her head while she remembers the brutal welcoming she received.

After been separated from her daughter and her husband, she was conducted to a train station and up to a grey train with worn out wagons. Women sobbed and cried loudly as they were cramped in the wagons like cattle. The space inside was so little; they were all catching for breath, sweating by the concentrated heat of too many bodies in a little space.

The trip took hours and several women fainted inside the wagons, leaning against the other women, while some little girls were crushed against the walls completely immobile.

Her legs became tired and her knees began to twitch. In the confined space, she couldn't move as freely as she was used to. She tried to move her feet by leaning against the door and she could stare at the beautiful scenery outside, green trees contrasting next to the creamy vast wheat crop fields. It wasn't an ugly country. There was something eerily sad about the whole anguish and despair they were all experiencing, and the strangely beautiful scenery of the country. Several small wooden houses painted in pastels colours and white fences, scattered in the land fields went by, as the train traveled through the empty lands of the country.

The train arrived at a white stone building, glistening under the blue skies of the Pacific coasts of that Amerikan country. When Anatoliy told her about the several trips they would have to do over the Amerikan country of Panama, she quickly looked it up realizing astonished of the beauty of the little country in the Caribbean. She dreamt of the white sand beaches with clear, greenish waters, the palm trees, and the wildlife. A perfect crowned sapphire in the middle of the continent. Alongside the astounding surroundings of the fauna of the country, the 3D renders of the resort complex Anatoliy planned to build at the coast of it, complimented each other like coconut and lime in a Caribbean cocktail.

She thought of all of that with careful attention as she stepped down the asphyxiating wagon of the train alongside the other scared women. In a zombie state, she crossed the gravel floors in front of the tall white building. She walked near the six huge romanic style columns of the porch. Soldiers conducted women to several tables separated in front of white tents. A crying girl screamed pleading not to be separated from her mother while a soldier had his gun pointing at her face. Chaos sprung all over and Natasha stared with a terrified look, how mothers were separated from their daughters and a high pitch pain struck her, with the remembrance of Sofy's face staring back at her when Sergeant Davis grabbed her from her arms.

They were lined up, and a soldier began checking them before forming them in front of the different tables with other soldiers typing down information on computers. One soldier looked at her with his bright blue eyes, inspecting her from head to toe, lifting her grey dress to look at her legs with an indecorous attitude. He rubbed his hands up and down her legs; making her jump astonish to the conduct of the soldier, but the man simply responded with a smile and cracked into laughs with the rest of his comrades; not before spanking her buttocks and leaving her to inspect another woman. After being preliminary inspected by the 'freehand soldier', they were instructed to form a line in front of each tent; she could count six, but there could be more. Terrified and feeling abused by the stranger's hand she walked to one of the tables where a soldier sat staring back at her behind golden spectacles. The man could be as old as Anatoliy, and his stern look was scary at times. She swallows nervously and clutches her hands in front of her, twitching her fingers with each hand.

"Name?!" the man asked as he stared at her expectantly.

"Na…Natasha Isayeva" she answered trying to fix her already messed up hair.

The man didn't say anything else and grabbed a grey piece of clothing and two little flat shoes. He lifts a plastic box and she gave one-step backwards confused with his actions. "Your jewels!" he ordered and she nervously started taking off the bracelet on her left wrist; and while she did that, she looked around and stared back at the different tables where other women were being subjected to the same treatment she was. She picked the hairpin that holds up her hair, making it waterfall down her back, and she gently rubbed the elaborated iris flower adorning it. She remembered the Christmas morning she opened the burgundy velvet box and the sunlight hitting the diamonds, amethysts, emeralds, and pearls of the hairpin. The hairpin fell on the plastic box heavily as she left it there and takes off the necklace around her neck; it fell inside the box with all its weight. The man started inspecting her jewellery as she strips down from all the opulence every piece gave to her.

She grabbed the clothes and the flat grey shoes and scarily looked around at everyone. Women were been inspected; mothers and daughters were separated and put in different groups according to their ages.

"Where do I change?" she asked the man who inspected her and he stared back at her with unwary looks. "Where do I change?" she asked again almost ordering him to tell her where to change her outfit.

"There!" pointing with his pen at the ground.

Her jaw dropped, stunned at the order.

"Now!" he yelled, urging her to change her outfit.

"Isn't there any private place where I could change?" she said worried at having to expose herself in front of everyone.

"Do it now or we will change you!"

"But..."

"I suggest you do it." A passing by woman told her fixing the grey suit and flipping her hair back. "The soldiers get a little handy" moving her fingers while raising her hand.

Natasha sighed and her eyes saddened. She carefully unbuttoned the cuffs of her dress, and slowly rolled down the zipper in the back. She swallowed saliva and look around for anyone staring at her, but no one was paying attention to her; everyone was busy with their own stuff. It was strange for her to go back to the place of help, as it has been a long time since she was in that position. Nervously her hands pulled the dress off the shoulders, baring her smooth skin to the air. Only Anatoliy has been the only one to see her expose body in that manner, and now she was forced to strip down of any coverage in public. Her heart faltered in the angst of being observed. Her whole surroundings seemed to have slow down so she could see every detail of the crooked smiles, the batting eyelashes, the laughs and impertinences of the Amerikan soldiers.

The grey dress fell on the muddy floor, while she tries to cover her bareness from everyone. Completely vulnerable she picked up the grey uniform and once she tried to put it on a soldier grabbed the clothes in his hands stopping her of any movement and told her to take her underwear off too. She pleads for compassion, but for the Amerikan's she was just another annoying Russian woman that wasn't obeying and who was being a pain to be processed. So the soldier ignored her plead, mocking her behaviour and turned around her, picks a pocketknife from his combat belt and reached to the soft lace of her underwear. The blade shone clean, as it travels to the encounter of the delicate silk lace and it forcefully ripped off the impeccable work of undergarment. She screamed at the cold touch of the blade and at the sudden exposure of her bareness. She fought in vain and fell on the floors, sobbing and covering her nude body. The soldiers started to make fun of her with no reservations or decorum, belittling her more and more.

"Private!" A distinguished man in impeccable black uniform approached them. Natasha could see her reflection over the perfectly polished shoes.

“Haha… – Lieutenant!” the man stood straight when his superior called for his attention.

The man kneeled in front of her and covered her naked body with the grey suit she was supposed to put on. All shaky, she put on the suit, staring frantically at the soldiers around them, while other women, in other tables, were being inspected and stripped away from any jewellery they had on themselves.

Sir?” she called out the lieutenant who ignored her walking away and looking down on everyone. “Sir?!” she reached out for his arm from behind, and all the soldiers jumped to his guard, lifting their guns; pointing at her. The lieutenant turned around and stares warmly and directly into her eyes. His brownish eyes were so inviting and so tender, she felt secure and confident he could help her in anything.

“Yes?” he asked softly and gently grabbed her hand from his arm, while with the other arm he signals everyone to put the guns down.

“Please, Sir. I beg of you to help me.”

“How can I help you?” he smiled.

“I shouldn’t be here – The…the…there must be a way where I get some better conditions…” she stuttered, “…I am from a noble family.” She almost cried.

“Lieutenant Samuels!” A woman in dark uniformed and carrying a tablet on her arms called him out from far away.

“Unfortunately Miss, I can’t help you right now.” He said losing the grip on his hand and before walking away towards the other woman, he studied Natasha’s body from head to toe.

A siren howled loudly, and she was transported back to reality.

“Time for work…again!” a woman complained as they all woke up from a night sleep.

"Nat" a woman kneeled before her and gently rubbed her shoulders. "You didn't sleep again last night, don't you?" She put her arm below Natasha's "C'mon I will help you." Helping her stand on her feet.

Like grey souls, they all walk through the cold barracks into the damped outside from all the pouring rain. The tiny flat shoes quickly thickened in mud as they cross the camps towards the vehicles where some soldiers waited for them to board. Prisoners of their own miserable lives, they all sat in rows of three and Natasha stared outside the window, completely lost in her thoughts. As the vehicle takes them to their workplace, she couldn't help but reminiscence on the green pastures of the outskirts of Moscow, the beautiful architecture of the city and the joyful giggles from Sofy while being ridden to their destination. Natasha knew poverty and hard work, but the forced labour days the Amerikans have imposed on all of them has worn out her spirit and hopes.

The vehicle reached the factory and they all began descending and walking towards the inside. Sadly, she dragged her shoes by the hand of her new friend, who tried to hide her estate from any of the privates. Vera found pitiful the way Natasha was for some weeks after been imprisoned. The concentration camps weren't a place for someone with the delicate ways and manners she displayed, and she also found empathy in the pain she suffered as she has lost a child before. She sits her carefully on her work stool in the production line and she sat next to her.

"There you go." She sighed. "You will see how your mind will wander off from everything once we start working." She said while staring at her empty eyes.

The soldiers started checking on every single one of them with spite and disgust. Two soldiers approached them and picked their heads up from their chins, inspecting the two from left to right.

“This one looks like shit!” the guy spit with a muffled smirk and with Natasha’s face on his hand.

“Nah, she is alright!” the other turned around and rubbed his crotch against her shoulder until his mouth was right next to her left cheek, and she could feel his hot breath hitting her skin. “I am sure that under all these rags it’s hidden a hot bod!” grasping her by her left breast.

“Leave her alone!” Vera protested hitting him on the arm with her tight fists.

“Keep out of this bitch!” the man slapped her with all his fury and strength. So hard that she felt on the floor, bleeding on the edges of her lips.

“Stop fooling around! We have to start the day!” another soldier yelled from far away.

The two men leave while blowing kisses at the two, making remarks on how they were like animals in need of real men to tame them.

Natasha grabbed her friend from the arm to help her up. She apologized but Vera said it was nothing, as she knows how hard it has been for her. She understood how painful it must be to know that your only child is out there somewhere. So near and yet so far away from your reach.

The production line started and once again, they found themselves assembling up little electronic parts, they have no idea what for.

● ● ● ● ●

In a great house with tall French-style windows, oak floors and Etruscan wallpaper; tea was being served in a perfect china set. Crystal chandeliers swung from side to side, from the slight gusts of wind that travelled through the corridors of the magnificent house. Fresh cut roses were set in vases over several rosewood tables and Eleanor turned on the radio with her gloved hands. The radio signals battle a little but it quickly picked up the station from the Ministry of Communications or MoC, of the Amerikan Empire with recent news of the advances of the empire. How the diplomatic negotiations have been going with the Western Soviet Empire and how the Ministry of Defense has doubled the ensemble of weapons provided to the army, to protect the Amerikan citizens. She felt proud of her empire; she took a sip of tea and crossed her legs rejoicing with the hymn of victory and strength, which served as a symbol for the cause of the Amerikan Empire.

"Esfir!" She called out, and a maid quickly walked in.

"Yes ma'am"

"It's Claudia in her room?" she questioned not even bothering on facing her maid.

"No ma'am, she is in the playroom right now. Would you like me to fetch her?" she asked with her head down and her hands twitching nervously.

"No!" She stood up. She slowly walked towards the door and when she was next to the maid she stops looking outside with her head held higher than she could. "Don't you ever dare to suggest me anything."

"But ma'am." The maid cried. "I…I…"

"Shut it!" she yelled and left the woman trembling with terror.

Her heels thumped against the wood as she walked across the hallways of the house.

Reaching a white door, she opened it and stood to stare at Sofy playing with a tea set on the floor. She smiled and suddenly she came to a halt when her boyfriend surprised her by hugging her from behind.

"You've got close to that little girl." Rubbing her shoulders, then sliding her hair uncovering her sleek neck and lovingly kiss her, making her smile.

“She is a cute pet.” She mentioned positioning her left hand over his cheek while he kept kissing her neck.

“You do know, you have to send her to Reform School.”

“Yes I will take her eventually to R.S.” she turned around and faced him. His hands fell around her waist while their bodies got tighter against each other. “I already rename her.” Said with an evil smile.

“Really? How do you name her?”

She turned around again facing back at Sofy, who played unaware of what was happening by the door. In her oblivious innocence, she felt content surrounded by toys, candy, and sweets. The man’s hands carefully descended from the top of her neck, travelling through her torso, inspecting every crevice, the plumpness of her breasts and the curves of her waist. She quivered by his touch and the indecency of the situation. Her lips parted, her skin began releasing tiny drops of sweat, when the zipper of her skirt was pulled down and one of his hands slipped inside. Her body clenched as she arches her back inviting him to touch her. She exhaled when his hand and fingers found safety between her thighs and his lips sucked on her neck.

“Claudia.” She moaned before biting her lower lip. “I name her Claudia”

Grisha stared at Rupert facing the garden through the tall windows of one of the corridors in Bellinski Manor. Rupert sat with a photograph in his hand, gazing in the empty space before him. The photographs and memory of Marci were too much to handle still. For Grisha, it wasn't understandable all the pain Rupert felt for the loss of a total stranger, and he wondered if he would feel the same if he suddenly disappears. His nails rubbed the glass from the window while the labourers move stuff around in the background. If only he knew the answer of what to do to help him; If only his presence was enough to make him get over Marci's memory.

A slight gust of wind hit Rupert's face and losing the grip from his hand, the photograph flew away, falling on the grass. He didn't move, nor bothered on looking for it. Grisha's shoes stopped at the small paper over the greenery. Silently he slowly kneeled and pick it up with a saddened look on his eyes and a couple letters on his hands. His shoes sank on the grass as he stepped towards the bench and towards Rupert's gloomy self.

"Don't do this to yourself." He said while sitting next to him. "You need to find a way to move on."

Rupert said nothing; his eyes looked empty. Grisha reached his hands, holding them tenderly.

"It's…" he broke his silent state. "It's hard to believe Nikolai did all of these."

"I know." Grisha's eyes tear a little listening to the pain in Rupert's voice. It was hard to imagine the once cocky and strong Rupert Bellinsky so broken down. His spirit seems to have crumbled completely; it seems that he could somehow accept the loss of Marci but not the betrayal from his best friend. "I find it difficult to believe it also."

"We are responsible also…" he said.

"Why would you say that?"

"Because we were the closest to him and somehow we never saw…we never sense something was going on with him…if only we knew…we could have done something…say something…"

"I don't think it was that simple to spot. Besides nobody is blaming us." Holding his head between his hands and staring into his eyes.

"I can't agree with you!" he shook his head from Grisha's embrace and standing he gave a few steps forward in the loan.

"Rupert." Grisha almost whispered his name, as the words escape from behind his lips, timid and lingering.

"It's all wrong." Rupert sighed looking down on the grass. Something so insignificantly to most people had become the main focus of his thoughts.

"Perhaps you could take your mind off from things slowly. I

noticed you haven't read any correspondence." Walking towards him with the letters in his hand offering them with a slight smile. Rupert knew he meant well. His eyes were warm, and everything about Grisha seemed covered by an angelical halo.

He took the letters, look around for the remittent, and suddenly realizes another of his fears hitting him hard.

"Are you ok?" Grisha asked leaning forward.

In frenzy, Rupert ripped the envelopes apart, releasing the letters and quickly read them one after another. The papers fell over the green loan as he went on reading the letters and as Grisha stared confuse at his inexplicable behaviour. Rupert's breath began to falter, and anxiety grew, his heart started to skip beats and his hands tighten, clenching the papers in his hands.

"My parents…" he faintly said in the desperate state he was. "They are in Amerika." Only saying that astounded him.

Stunt, Grisha kneeled picking up the papers and gave them a quick look while Rupert stood frozen in place, with his eyes tearing a little and a slight tremble went through his whole body. The fear of his own parents in the middle of the whole war was maddening and even though he was quite independent, their loss would significantly be tough for him.

Taking a deep breath, "Look at the dates…perhaps they are no longer there."

"I don't believe that."

"We've got to hope for that, or at least for them to be away from any danger."

"I need a drink." Rupert stormed towards the house leaving Grisha behind, holding the letters and an anguish pain, crushing his heart by seeing his friend and lover suffering.

• • • • •

Waves hit the hull of the ship while we are taken away and a rattling steel chain clung from far away due to the movement. It might have seemed it was easy for Krysi and me to be here on our way to a new life, when in fact it really wasn't. After saving her from the hands of the crazy Aryana, I stared at myself on the mirror of the bathroom with her blood splattered over my face. I ran the cold water and began washing the blood off my hands. I looked back at Krysi lying on the bed and my brown eyes glimmered with the steel blue shades of the night. After cleaning up, I wrapped her in very warm blankets, and held her in my arms, leaving the sinister scene.

Through the cobbled streets and between the walls of the buildings, I strolled with Krisy in my arms. Reaching the bar, I knocked on the door and waited for someone to open it. It was very late at night, but with the hotel transformed into a crime scene, I didn't have any other place to go. I waited for what it seemed like a long time. I could hear the steps of peace agents nearer and nearer. I closed my fist tight and as I was about to knock again, even louder than I have before, a light lit up in the inside; and I sighed in relieve once I saw it, releasing the grip of my fist.

"What are you doing here?"

"I know is late. I'm really sorry." I said agitatedly. "I need to hide somewhere."

The voices from the peace agents came louder as they approached the corner near the bar, and I glanced over stressed out and anxious. The old man stared at me. He looked at Krysi in my arms and noticed small bloodstains on the collar of my shirt. He shook his head and let me in. He turned off the light and we both stood still, holding our breathes as we saw the blurry images of the peace agents walking pass the windows of the bar, the lights from the weapons flashing on every direction.

"Follow me." He guided me to the basement.

Once there I let myself loose, sitting on the floor resting my back against a wooden box and I sighted relieved on having my girl safe once again.

"I will call Anichka." The man said standing by the stairs.

Minutes later, she sat in front of me thinking carefully on what to do now. I somehow changed all the plans she already had for smuggling us abroad.

"First you need to get the money." She stared at me seriously.

"I know, I should have thought about that before coming here… but I had her with me…and…" I said brushing Krysi's hair.

"I got it." She said, "We can't let more time to go by."

"I agree…I just…"

"I'll take care of her while you look for it and your stuff." She interrupted me before I could even ask for help.

I was worried about leaving my precious daughter with another stranger once again, but I didn't have any other choice. I walked out, back into the dark streets avoiding any peace agent that were making rounds all around. I perhaps had to thank the owners of such a low-key hotel, for the lack of guests they had, cause I wouldn't have been able to get through a police infested site. When I got there, it was untouched, unmoved. Aryana's dark trail of victims lay on the exact same spot I left them. Then a slight sob came to me from behind the main desk of the lobby, and I remember I left a woman trapped in the pantry room at the back. I stood for a couple of seconds considering whether I should let her go free or leave her there once again. I had mixed feelings with the polarizing life I'm having so far.

I wanted to take Krysi away from all the death, the rot and the pain, I had caused too many people including myself. I looked at the stairs leading up and listen to the empty building.

"I can't let you go," I muttered to myself with pain in my heart against the door, my breath hitting the surface. As much as I wanted to change things and I wanted things to be different this time; I couldn't risk any more my precious girl.

I could hear the whimpering fade behind me as I walked up through the stairs and walked towards my room. I grab everything I could and back onto the streets towards the bar. I felt my heart was rising with every step I gave. I wasn't sure about leaving Krysi with Anichka, as I almost lose her because of my careless behaviour and my unhealthy desire for the hunt. My eyes watered under the cold and gentle wind that blew against my face. I haven't sleep properly lately. As I pass next to the window of a building, a glowing white figure caught my attention from the corner of my eye, but when I look at towards its direction, it disappeared instantly. A strange sensation travelled through my senses as if I have seen that ghostly figure before roaming my life.

Back at the bar, I found to my relieve Anichka with Krysi. Perhaps there are still people out there I could trust; certainly, I could trust this woman.

"You brought the money?" she asked handing me, my girl.

I look inside the pockets of my coat and handed her the small velvet bag containing the precious gems, "Is that enough?"

"More than enough." Her eyes widened surprised at the number of stones in it. Of course, they weren't all; I couldn't dare to spend everything on one trip. I needed to be smart and kept some for myself secretly safe in a small wallet.

"I will call my guy…we have to act as fast as we can." She turned around and began making phone calls while I waited patiently with Krysi on my arms. I leaned back against some boxes and rest my eyes while I listened to Anichka make different arrangements through her phone.

Fire exploded in front of my eyes while a fire breather performer entertained different people. I looked down on krysi but she wasn't there. In fact, I was dressed differently. I was once again wearing one of my many elegant suits and then gaze around at the party, and everyone was having a merry fun, drinking and laughing. I haven't lost track of time, so I knew this wasn't real; I knew it more, as I would have never separated myself from Krysi without being aware of it, and this scene felt so familiar, a lost memory imprinted on my mind. A gentle touch on my shoulder made me turned around to see my beloved Josephine standing behind me with a huge smile on her face. Another dream where I could reencounter myself with her and my eyes filled slightly with tears as her hand poses graciously itself on my cheek. I close my eyes feeling the warmth from her delicate hand. Slowly her hand started to clench her fingers against my face for no apparent reason. The melody from the orchestra was loud and steady and the soothing notes of the harmony was opposing to the tight grip from Josephine's hand. Her nails started to sink into my flesh with intent but without hurting me. I could feel her body getting close and her face almost near mine. I could smell her sweet perfume and slowly felt her other hand on my face and now she had my face in between her hands. Her lips gently rested over mine and she pressed against them, kissing me passionately. I couldn't resist myself, my hands went around her waist, and they travelled up her back, caressing the lace of her dress and pulling her tighter to my body. Then the kiss stopped.

"I knew you didn't love me," Beatrice said and my eyes opened stunned. Her nails tight in the flesh of my face and with a tight grip and I couldn't move. My body tensed and I try to move my head away but I couldn't without her nails sinking deep in my face.

"I won't let go!" she whispered as she leans her face very near mine and instinctively I pushed away and blood began dripping from the wounds created by her nails, and a piercing pain came from all the wounds. Anichka's boot hitting my leg woke me up from the strange dream.

"Wake up sleeping beauty!" she said looking down at me with her bothered eyes.

Krysi played around with some potatoes and carrots rolling them on the floor oblivious to what was about to be spoken. I stood up and saw a man about my height and complexion, standing in the room with us. The man turned around and it was as if he could be my twin. Not exact, but close enough to pass as myself, as I would find eventually; long enough for us to be able to run off without being followed.

"The resemblance is uncanny, right? We had to dye his hair and add several prosthetics to his face to resemble you more." Anichka said circling around the man who stood to stare at me.

To me, it was as if my past was judging every inch of my skin, the stubble beard, the worn out clothes. He wasn't wearing anything fancy, but it was as if I try too hard to be unnoticed that I look even worse than a poor man.

"He will give himself away and we will drive away from the town while he diverts all the attention on him." She said looking at me.

"Does he know what to do?" I asked

"He's been briefed. He is ready."

"I don't..." the man said and I squint my eyes as he spoke, "I don't believe this is correct..." he gave three steps forward towards me with a menacing sight on his eyes. Anichka took a grip on the gun from her belt. "You killed a lot of innocent people…I am doing this cause I need the money." Almost spitting into my face.

I turn my face to the side disgusted by his hypocrisy. Then I looked back at him into his eerie similar eyes from mine and said nothing. There wasn't any answer I could give to this man that would make him change any point of view about me; He was right, I am a murderer and he is supposed to save me.

"When are we leaving?" I asked Anichka, who gently let go the grip from the gun.

"Soon."

We exchanged personal papers and we got new identities. The other Nikolai walked out the bar and towards the train station packed with peace agents holding big guns and with the blue holographic posters with my face displayed all over. He walked past the first set of peace agents without any of them stopping him.

"You should walk right in front in a couple of minutes," Anichka said.

"Why?"

"That way you will appear in the surveillance without being the primary subject, and we will rule out the persona you are now."

So, without asking anything more, I walk past the train station, while people gather around and took their mobile devices to take photographs of what was going on inside the station. I felt uneasy looking at my face in the glowing blue holographic posters. It was a surreal image in slow motion, to see myself been dragged out of the train station by several peace agents around me. The man lifted his head and gave me a scorned look and I step back behind the crowd that gathered around to watch the devious minister taking in the custody of the peace agents.

I followed Anichka back to a cargo vehicle with Krysi on my hands and holding my bags. It was finally over. I was on my way to a new start. The cargo vehicle drove away from the town, and I slowly remember everything that has happened here in the last couple of days as we pass near Aryana's house, the hotel, and the café.

EIGHT

The buzzing sound of the hair clipper as it goes all over her head haunted Natasha's mind. In fact was one of the many sounds that haunted her existence, besides the screams and cries from the women and child she has encountered in the short period of time she is been imprisoned. Yet she still remembers the smile of her daughter, her husband's gentle touch on her right cheek and his tender and loving kiss. The barracks were cold, and they all struggle to keep their bodies healthy.

Natasha looked at her decrepit reflection on a glass window in the factory. Her cheeks sunken, as well as her eyes, looking dark and tired. Her eyes watered a little in the sadness contemplation of her new self. Her radiant skin, luscious locks and the lively glimmer from her eyes have almost disappeared.

"You! Go back to work." A private yelled at her from behind.

She steps away from the window and walks back to her seat next to Vera; back to the production line of the strange metal pieces. An alarm rung announcing a break for the ladies to stretch their legs and eat a small piece of bread and a cup of coffee. They all walked out into the fenced courtyard and after standing in long lines to get their small meal, they walked around the perimeter of the factory grounds, like in a huge maximum-security prison. The doomed ghosts eat and drank the miserable food they were given, and yet one singular soul wasn't eating at all. Natasha sat on the stairs looking at the grandeur outside the fence, thinking about her family, her long-gone life, but wanting desperately for her life to end. Vera looked at her with a broken heart. She tried, to at least, get something in her stomach. Telling her it wasn't worth wasting her life that way because she never knew when the troops would come and save them from their captivity and she will finally reunite with her daughter. That single idea gave her enough hope to find courage inside her heart.

A woman collapsed a couple of meters in front of them. The coffee splashed against the gravelled ground, the small piece of bread rolled away and her body laid on the floor still. Some of the girls nearby run towards the body, turned her around and check her vital signs. Privates ran as they found the commotion and kicked the woman, yelling at her to stand up persistently. When the woman didn't respond, they dragged her away and the alarm rang again calling for the end of the break.

"You think she will be fine?" some of the women talk to each other.

"I doubt she will. – She wasn't responding at all."

"Where are they taking her?"

Everybody had more questions than answers as they walked back to their workstations. A couple of hours later, nobody remembered about the woman or the fact she was dragged away like a piece of meat across the gravelled floor.

The front doors of the factory open while they kept working on their stations inadvertently to all of them. Suddenly, the production line stopped and they look at each other surprised. That hasn't really happened since they got there; it was the first time.

"Everybody, we are going to make a medical assessment." A female private said through a speaker from an office above them all. Natasha looked down at her left wrist and stares at the number tattooed on it and the pain of the needle going through her skin burnt her. In these countries far from home, the weather was unpredictable; it could be sunny in one minute and in the next minute, a thunderstorm rage outside over everybody's head. The Amerikans didn't care that much about any of them; for them, they were cattle, scum, and filth. A searing rain started to pour above their tired souls as they waited in lines to be medically assessed. The water felt cold against their skins, the grey linen dresses soaked and stuck to their bodies, puddles grow around the gravel and several cadets walked around them with their guns ready while keeping them submissive. Dirt splashed against their exposed ankles as they walk a few steps forward the line.

Strangely, the water pouring down Natasha's body didn't really bother her. It actually reminded her of when she was a little girl, dreaming big about becoming someone important.

"It must have been because of that woman," Vera said leaning in Natasha's ear from behind.

A familiar face appeared from behind the medical team under a black umbrella. He looks strong and elegant, even on these conditions, his commanding composure gave Natasha an eerie vibe. It was almost as he was inspecting her from afar. The medical team take look at them; check their breath, skin, their eyes, and their teeth. Some women were pulled aside and the rest were told to go back to their workstations. Natasha shivered after standing under the rain for several minutes and couldn't help but feel conscious about her scrawny body, when the medic pulled her dress up, as he revised her, exposing her body to the elegant man. It wasn't the first time he saw her naked, but now she was more vulnerable. She coughs and the medic looked at her concern about the coughing, and as he was about to file her as unhealthy, the lieutenant walked towards them, took his jacket off and covered her shivery body.

"These women need more food." He said with his hands over Natasha's shoulders. She felt them heavy, but warm and protected for the first time in a long time.

"We have rationalized the portions while the crops grow." His assistant mentioned while trying to cover him with the black umbrella.

"Why was that? There wasn't any real reason to cut down the portions; there was enough food in the stock facilities." He complained.

"It was an administrative decision, sir."

"That can't be. Find more food for these women!" He grabbed his jacket from Natasha and walked away, "We can't afford to lose any more of these women! They are big assets for our cause!" he stormed off.

Natasha felt the weight of the jacket taken off her shoulders and the cold weather hit her body strongly like sharp needles, making her shiver slightly. After they were all medically assessed, they returned to their labours, twisting screws and assembling unknown parts to each other.

● ● ● ● ●

"I told you a walk in the city would make you good," Grisha said while walking down the streets of their beloved city, which was starting to slowly bloom once again. Buildings were being repaired and businesses were being open again; Things seem to have gone back to a certain normality. Still, on the news the horrors of the concentration camps from afar could be seen, complains against the incapacity of the Empire dealing with the Amerika's situation was the outburst in the whole country. Europa became a strong political ally to the Amerikan Empire, and suddenly the Asian Nations were in negotiations to take down the ultimate power of the Russian crown. Many enemies came along with great power, and to the Russian crown, it was a long history. Always seen as a threat, never more than now, when almost all control fell upon their lap.

Rupert nodded while looking at children playing knives on the ground. He could see himself playing knives with his father when little and a slight smirk showed in his face. "Let's have a drink." He said pointing at a nearby bar.

The place was full of men talking politics and war. Everyone was tense with the whole situation. A young uniformed man burst in, followed by several others carrying flyers on their hands, as Rupert ordered two glasses of sherry. Grisha turned to look at them while the clientele of the place kept chatting loudly; saying what the government has to do and what not to on a situation like this, and the faults of the politicians and even questioning whether or not they need to be ruled by an emperor. It was considered treason to speak ill of any of the royal family, but in times like this, a law like that was less enforce, as everyone was in discontent. People talk in a response to the stress they were living in, and no one could blame a poor citizen to complain and curse the crown when they are uncertain of their own future.

"Gentlemen, please! –" The officer said "We do nothing by just standing here drinking our souls and complaining. We have to take action!" everyone silenced. He was speaking the plain truth. We as a society have not changed much from our ancestors; we all talked a lot but when it turns for us to do something, to take some action to change things, we do nothing. We all expect others to do the deeds and we enjoy the comforts of someone else's fight or complain if that fight does not succeed. The other uniformed men gave out flyers and they got one each. Grisha looked down at the white paper with bold black letters asking for new cadets to join the forces.

"We camc here because we are on recruit tour for new members for our army." The man said. "Who of you gentlemen will fight to gain back our way of living? – Who of you will fight for a future for our children, our families – for ourselves?"

The men look at each other and some look away, avoiding having eye contact with any of the uniformed men. An old man with a grey beard stepped forward and said aloud he would join the forces and everybody stood silent.

"Thank you Sir – Are you young men going to let old men fight for you?"

"Maybe we should step out," Grisha smirked grabbing Rupert by his forearm.

Rupert's feet planted straight in the ground of the bar, and Grisha felt his heart sinking with the realization of what he wouldn't ever want to happen.

"I will enroll." Rupert turned around and whispered to him.

"You can't – you are not thinking straight." Looking back at him with saddened eyes.

It's something I have to do!" he stared back with determination on his eyes. Grisha stood frightened as Rupert steps forward towards the uniformed men.

Other men approached them too to enroll themselves to the forces and with pain in his heart, Grisha stared as Rupert signed his name and pledged his life to the crown. In all the commotion, Grisha felt time slowing down and tragedy sunk in his soul; the ideas of losing Rupert all of a sudden stroke him hard, and quickly his eyes move fast as he thought on ways to persuade him from putting himself in danger. However, it was already late, the men cheered for the new recruits and they all escorted them to the outside where a big army truck waited for them, to drive them directly to the training camps; there was no time to waste. Before he could step up the car, Grisha pulled Rupert aside looking distressed, almost about to cry out his love for him.

"I have to do this," Rupert said and against anyone's judgement, he placed his right hand on Grisha's left cheek. "Please understand."

Grisha's eyes watered as he closed them feeling the warm touch of his lover's hand against his cheek. Could this be the last time they are this close? Could this be the last day they stare into each other's eyes? Feel each other's heartbeat? He sighed, resigned and fighting to understand the reasons Rupert has to go to war.

"Promise me you will come back."

"I promise you…" he said leaning in, to almost kissing him in front of all the men, who actually didn't care or mind about them. The tragedy of war has put many things into perspective. Love was meant to be expressed, and life was so short and so fragile to be judging and pointing fingers on others without caring about your own stuff. Hypocrisy was a story from the past. Even though they were going to war; love, care, and tolerance filled everyone's hearts. "…This won't last for long." He walked towards the truck, holding hands with Grisha.

"Don't fail me…I…" Grisha said as their grip cut loose and their hands separated. His voice broke as he realized that at this moment he would actually tell Rupert for the first time that he loved him. It took too much time for him to make terms with his mind, as Rupert sat down and the truck started driving away; Grisha stood in the street looking at it go, while a cold wind blew against his face and slight tears fell from his eyes with his hopes of a happy life with the man he loves. "I love you." He whispered.

Heavy sweat ran down Anatoliy's back while he works with several other men in crop fields at a concentration camp. His former self was long gone now. His eyes looked tired and sported dark circles underneath them, his cheek sunk into his skull, his hair became brittle and his hands filled with callouses; his whole spirit got broken when he was brought in that camp. Cramped in the suffocating trains, older men peed and released their bowels while waiting to arrive at their destiny, soiling the small space they shared and filling it all with a nauseous stench.

With their thin physiques, they were forced to work repeatedly under the burning sun, denied water constantly and expected to work as hard as their bodies could. It was proved constantly through lashings and beatings, to old and young equally, when some of them couldn't resist the intense labour. Rainy days brought a different struggle to all of them, who had to battle with not falling ill with a cold, or even freezing to death by the extreme weather and the lacks of warm clothes. Being constantly assessed by medical teams, they didn't know exactly what happens to the ones they all clearly knew were ill. Once you fell ill, no one would ever see you again. So for everyone was a struck of luck to be found healthy, or at least healthier than the ones considered ill.

"We have to find a way out." A man muttered while sitting next to Anatoliy during a meal break.

"It's not simple." Another one said.

"There must be something we could do."

"He speaks the truth," Anatoliy said now joining the conversation. "We are being watched all the time; these men are not going to be easy to fool."

They all look up at the fence in the far distance.

"If only we could go through that electric fence." One of them mentioned taking a bite of the dry and stale piece of bread.

"It's risky. We could end up fried as Vlad, stuck to the wired fence." Other mentioned, and they all remember. Vlad was a man who tried his luck on escaping. Luck wasn't on his side as he desperately ran through the wet grass on a misty night. He looked back to the buildings as he ran forward towards the fence and with an agile move he jumps with all his strength and his hands grabbed the wire in a tight grip.

Sparks flew instantly when his hands were exposed to the electric wires, his body shook violently, smoke began to grow as his flesh was burning and turning itself carbonized black. His heart stops and his breath left his body as if he felt finally free from all the torturous life they were living.

"Desperation is a bad counsellor," Anatoliy said.

Vlad's body remains there as a reminder to anyone of the consequences of trying to jump the fence. Several times, they take groups there to have a look at the maggot-filled corpse, inflicting fear on all of them. Crows and vultures have eaten a lot of flesh out and parts of his skull began to show from the side of his head, while a couple of fingers were missing. The body barely attached to the fence, and you could clearly see that wild animals had been feeding on the 'cooked' escaper. The gruesome view could give the strongest man chills and fear down his spine.

The siren rung again and some of the soldiers came around signaling them to go back to work, and silently they all walk back to the crops under the inquisitive sight of the Amerikan soldier's yoke. Long gone were the days in which Anatoliy spent his time doing leisure activities, servants carrying out the hard work and he didn't have to do anything for himself. Long gone were the days in which he was in command of his own life, in command of others and people had to obey him. Now every night he brushes his fingers against each other, feeling the callous skin of his worn out hands. His skin almost peeling off on certain places of the palms of his hands and his throat got a tight noose while he reminiscences his life. His perfect life.

One day, as he worked on the fields alongside other men, three soldiers called out six of them including him. Reluctantly they gathered in front of the uniformed men as they stare back at them, looking carefully at their physiques.

"These ones will work." The one with the scar under his eye said, looking annoyed at the task.

"But those two are old!" one said.

"I don't care." The scarred one said spitting on the ground. "They look strong enough for what they are needed."

"Walk on then! – or are you waiting for an invitation?" another one pointed with his gun at the six men whom stared at them almost shaking.

Their legs struggle to move forward because of the fear they had of the unknown task they were going to ask. The rest of the prisoners looked at them some with fear, others unmoved about their fate, and some with certain empathy towards their comrades, as none of them was meant to be imprisoned.

● ● ● ● ●

A maid dresses Claudia in a little girl's school uniform, with a grey pleated skirt surrounding her tiny legs, a white shirt and a black jacket with turquoise details, white long socks, and black Charolaise shoes. Her hair was pulled up in a small ponytail and two tiny pearl earrings adorned her lobes.

"She is ready ma'am." The maid said with the little girl by her hand and standing in the dining while Eleanor ate a bowl of fresh fruits for breakfast.

She turned her face to the girl, whose eyes twinkle, worried about not pleasing the stranger woman. Pushing the chair away, she stood and walked towards them silently.

"You look so beautiful." Kneeling in front of her, inspecting every detail of the uniform, "You will make a lot of friends today." She said.

"Is the car ready?" now she asks the maid with a scorned look in her eyes as if she was disgusted by her presence there.

"Yes, ma'am…" her voice trembled. "The driver is waiting."

She gently stood up, holding Claudia's little hand and staring back at the maid she hissed "I don't care if he is waiting." with fire in her eyes, and the girl lowered her face. "Take her to the car and wait for me!" she finally said looking with disdain at the young maid before leaving the dining room to wash her teeth and gather her black leather handbag.

Crossing behind huge black iron fences, the car went into the R.S. institute of the town. The three-story building resembled more a prison than a school; with tall glass windows, grey walls, all squared and no special details in the outside. Claudia's eyes were open wide as the car pulled in the courtyard of the school. Going through the hallways, Claudia looked at the murals and photographs across the walls, following Eleanor's lead; until they reached the principal's office in the top floor of the building. They walk in and they could see how the school was layout in the shape of a squared 'O', with an inner garden playground, divided into courts; sports, children, garden, and leisure.

"Elle!" A man walked in the office extending his arms towards Eleanor and hugged her warmly. "I am glad you finally decided to bring little Claudia to our Institute."

"Spencer." She whispered blushing as the man's hands grabbed her arms with their warmth touch. "Isn't she precious?" she asked pushing Claudia towards the center of the two.

His hand caressed down Claudia's brown locks and his fingers travelled down her cheeks and to her chin, lifting her head and her eyes shone right back at him, twinkling with innocence. "Indeed she is precious." He said.

Spencer's assistant walked in to lead Claudia to her class and left them alone in the office.

The group Claudia was assigned to have only ten children, and Principal Ashley's assistant sat her on the floor in the middle of the class with the rest of the children. The classroom was filled with toys, craft materials and small tables pushed towards the walls. The teacher brought her clay and began explaining the activity they were doing. As there was a slight language barrier, between the children and her, it took some time for all of them to understand the activity of modelling the clay in the shape of cardinal numbers. With her tiny and chubby fingers, Claudia grabbed a piece of blue clay and began shaping it into a number 1.

Back in the principal's office, Eleanor quivers under the scandalous touch of her lover Sergeant Ashley, as his hands travelled down her exposed back. Their relationship has never been stronger since the incursions in Russian soil.

"Please tell me you haven't taken interest on that girl because of Claudette." He asked looking up at the ceiling of his office while she lays naked on top of him.

She lifts her body and looked down at him, "Would you blame me?" she asked back.

"I just don't think is healthy."

"She would be her age now. I can't help but imagine our Claudette would look just like her." She said. Her dishevelled hair gave her a childish and unpolished look, while her eyes transmitted a longing for her lost child.

"I know." He caresses her cheek tenderly.

Then, wrapping his arms around her, he embraces her down to his chest and she rests her head on it. His hands brush her hair lovingly and as he does that, she sighs relaxed.

● ● ● ● ●

With a scorned look, a female cadet woke Natasha and the other women prisoners from their hard-earned sleep. Once again, she had another dream with her precious Sofy. She couldn't help but think of her wellbeing while walking towards the showers, and under the cold water, as she washes her bony physique with a tiny bar of soap. As her hands travelled down her sides, she could still remember the feeling of Anatoliy's hands on her and the deceive she concocted.

"Natasha! – Natasha!" Krystina Isayeva calls upon her desperately from her bedroom in the grandeur of Isayev House.

"Yes madam…" she walked in and gasped surprised with the horrific view.

"Don't you stand there, silly girl!" – Krystina cried – "Help me!" her hands were tinted with her own blood and a huge reddish puddle was forming on the bed, staining the bed sheets and her lacy nightgown.

After several minutes of waiting, dr. Kozlovsky walked out of the bedroom with a saddened look on his face, and Anatoliy, Nikolai, and Natasha knew immediately the bad news to come. Nikolai walks in the bedroom and sees his mom resting peacefully on her bed, while his father and Natasha sends the doctor away.

The months that followed that fateful night were a nightmare. Krystina came on and off from chronic depression. She barely ate, and Natasha felt empathy towards her and paid close attention to her needs. Anatoliy felt content with her service and more and more she was around and needed at home.

"This is your chance dumb girl!" Natasha's mom said while she gets Krystina's medicine from a chemist. "You are already close – you said that lady won't be able to carry any more children – but you could, and with that, they will be extremely grateful – they will pay you huge amounts of money." Her eyes were crazy and determined. "It could be your salvation." She sighs.

"Hurry, we have to get ready!" Vera rushes her back into the present and she quickly puts on her raggedy clothes and shoes. This was no life. She sacrificed a lot to earn the position Krystina Isayeva had, and now, it all slipped through her fingers. It was all a memory.

They formed rows outside the camp. They were supposed to be transported back to the factories as every day, but no movement of transportation was done. Something was happening. Several militia cars went in the camp from the far corner, going through a couple of buildings designed specially to harbour the female Russian prisoners. They could only hope for the men to be at least treated the same way. She could see rows and rows of women of all ages outside the six buildings where they were kept. The eldest woman could be sixty, barely; and the youngest could be sixteen. The cars went in front of all of them slowly driving the rocky road, and then, a lustrous black car pulled in right in front of them. The sun began to shine strongly above them, and sweat started to show on their foreheads and necks. Natasha felt her eyes wobbling and her breath started to falter. She wasn't strong enough to handle the difficulties of being exposed in extreme weather for extended periods of time. It was too hot, too humid, and too tough; and adding to that, the lack of nutrients consumed from the disgusting meals they were given.

The backdoor of the car opened, and a cold gust of air rushed towards them, as they saw Lieutenant Aiden Samuels stepped out of it. Natasha stared at his shiny black shoes, his impeccable uniform and his strong physique. He commanded power with his presence and taking off his dark sunglasses, his eyes blinked at her making her remember the tenderness and warmth she felt the first time she saw them. So inviting, so generous. But it was what she felt he transmitted to her with his sight.

"Lieutenant?" a female cadet stood next to him expectantly.

"I want her." He said and his voice was deep and manly.

Natasha felt her body wobbly, still affected by the heat and the deprivation from important nutrients. The female cadet walked towards her and pushed her forward; almost making her fell from all the dizziness.

"What's your number?" she asked as she stood in front of lieutenant Samuels, staring back with her lost eyes into his.

She lifts her arm and looks down at the number tattooed on her wrist. With the other hand, she brushed her fingertips over the printed number in grey ink. The strong heat from the machine was imprinted in her mind as she reminded of the time she was branded like an animal when firstly brought in the camps.

"3007" she muttered. Her eyes stared with blurry vision over the slight ridges of her wrist and hand.

"Louder!" the cadet yelled leaning on her ear, making her tremble.

"3007" she raised her voice.

The lady looked her up on her tablet and gave it to lieutenant Samuels to verify her identity, and after he reads the file, he told the cadet to prepare her and to take her to his residence; she was the one he was looking for. He turned around, got in the car and left the camps.

As Natasha was escorted alone to the showers in the barrack, the rest of the prisoners were back to the buses and to the factories. Two girls were pulled alongside Natasha and Vera turned her head back to look at her friend being taken in, surrounded by the uniformed cadets and feared went through her mind, wondering what was about to happen to her.

"Strip down!" the female officer ordered angrily.

She took off her worn shoes, putting her feet on the grey tiled floor of the showers, cold and wet from the past early showers. Under the sight of the cadets and the two other girls, she slowly stripped down from her raggedy and dirty clothes. Then, it was as if she has gone back in time. The two girls were ordered to shower her, and she felt the four hands from the girls around her as they cover her skin with rose scented soap. And, in the gentle movement from the choreographed scene for the soldiers, she looks up to the ceiling and closes her eyes, staring at the small crack openings on it filtering sunlight in. She could sense her maid showering her and the aroma of freshly boiled tea, and the sweet scent from mini cakes and a macaroons platter near her. She was then taken under the faucet and the soap was cleaned off, but lost in her memories, she diverts in the scent of her perfume bottles, her reflection as she applies makeup and the shimmering jewellery around her neck, wrists and ears.

● ● ● ● ●

I could still remember the feeling of Anichka's men fear as we waited patiently for her to return with the details of our sailing trip away from Russia, while I look outside the round window on the wall of the hull of the ship. I could barely make out my reflection on the glass window, but what I saw wasn't the same man whom I used to be; It was as if, everything I've done hasn't brightened me. Instead, a gloomy halo from an obscure world surrounded me. I know it was the right decision, taking Krysi away, but I long for the beauty of death I have given up for her.

"He does not look that terrifying – Be careful dumbass! You don't want to be another victim of the beheader." Some of Anichka's men spout while we sailed.

"Shut it!" she ordered.

"Don't listen to them." Then she said walking near me and sitting next to me with her back against the hull.

"The beheader, huh?!" I sighed at the foolish name given to me by a sensationalist news media.

"Why did you do it?" She asked me as we sat silently.

"Why?" I muttered looking down at my hands. Fixating in the

dryness of my skin, and carefully staring at the ridges of every centimeter of it. “Because of love.” I finally said.

She stared back at me unmoved.

“Love does not turn a gentleman into an assassin.”

“How do you know?” I said hoarsely, lifting my sight and looking directly into her eyes. The predator in me knew she shivered slightly and the hairs in the back of her neck stood. She was a strong woman, but still, my power of inflicting fear among anyone seem to be stronger.

“Because love is love – it doesn’t harm anyone, no matter what,” she answered determined. Perhaps it was the idealist in her, the same idealist who understands my desperate need to protect my daughter, to save her from my former life and self.

“It was true love…” I look away inside the lace of Krysi’s blanket. “True love makes you do things you never thought you were capable of; when true love does not correspond, it transforms into an incurable bleeding wound in your soul, your heart pounds so strong it hurts and you lose yourself trying to figure out what to do next with your life.”

We sat silently for a couple of seconds. It wasn’t simple to explain. I was a good man drawn into darkness, and in the end, I loved the strength it gave me. I mourn for that man I look in the mirror every day; I mourn for the man that was before the reflection, and for the lives, it has ended.

“Going to the dark path of life is easy…staying on the light one, it’s much harder…but trying to emerge from the darkness, leaving it behind, takes a lot of grit and courage.” She said leaning in and grabbing my hand. She could sense I was battling inside with the darkness in my soul and the light my daughter gives me and deserves to get in return.

“Boss! You got to see this!” a man called her out, and as we emerged from the insides of the ship into the deck, we saw several naval ships scattered in the distant waters.

"Brits." She muttered. "Let's hope they let us travel safely through their waters."

A small boat with the flag of Europa approached to our tiny ship, as we sail nearer and nearer. The captain called for the anchor to drop and suddenly our ship came into a stop. Some men from the crew helped the officials get over our ship and our captain walked out to the deck. I sat patiently with Krysi in my hands, feeling the gentle movements of the waves slightly moving the ship.

"Gentlemen! What can we do for you?" Our captain greeted the men.

"We need to see your registry – Captain…?"

"Captain Goraya – Borysko Goraya." He answered giving the registry records of the ship.

The man scanned the information and verified its authenticity. His brown eyes moved up to the captain and down again to the registry, and the pale skin on his face was slightly illuminated by the bluish tones of it. "It's all good – we will just make a quick inspection." He said signaling his crew to look around with his head.

When two of them came down, I stared at them silently and still; we've come this far in the trip and I have to avoid any attention towards me. They look around and opened some crates, and Krysi looked at me scared, her eyes almost into the edge of crying.

"Everything ok my love?" Anichka walked down and leaned towards Krysi. It surprised me and the men look at each other. The presence of a young baby girl in a cargo ship was suspicious, but thanks to the quick thinking from Anichka, they somehow understood she was the mother of the child; and perhaps we seemed like a family. A working family. Before they leave one of the men looked at me strangely, it was as if he knew who I was. His dark complexion was outstanding in comparison to mine. I was strong before, but now I was only a fragment of whom I was, and this man was the epitome of youth and strength. He looked at me with his hazel eyes, as if we had some connection. But I've never seen the man before, yet something pulled him to wonder at my face.

"Weston, let's go!" the other man called, distracting him from his weird stare.

Weston? It can't be. It was almost as if he could feel Marci's ghost behind my back, as if he could know I was the one who killed her. My eyes watered a little and I swallow saliva thinking on how the things we do in life and the people we touch, good or bad, linger around ourselves; like misty ghosts in the darkness, waiting to cry out the truth to anyone. I held my daughter tightly, feeling how she curled up against my chest. I needed her and the peace she provided.

● ● ● ● ●

The ride towards the military base camp was bumpy, and Rupert glanced at each of his companions inside the dark trunk of the truck. Across him, a young man stared back at him and he immediately recognized him as one of his servants. He then looks through a small hole in the tarp covering them and he could see the gloomy and ghostly scene outside. Even though the city was working hard to prove themselves that they could rebuilt their lives after the Christmas attack, the outskirts pretty much look like a grey land, where almost nothing wanted to grow or survive.

His black leather boots splashed on a muddy puddle outside the base, as he steps down the truck and they all waited for orders. All men looked around expectantly of what was coming next for them.

"Ladies!" A uniformed man yelled at them. "My name is Lieutenant Petrov and I'm in command of all your weak asses for the time determined for your service. You think you are all brave and fearless, but you are far from that. You are just a bunch of girls…a bunch of delicate girls!" he yelled screaming at them, almost spitting at them angrily. "Don't worry, we will turn you into men soon, proud of using this uniform…" hitting his chest effusively. "But first, we will break you in order to make you."

Slowly they were been dragged to a building where they were asked to strip down and dress up in grey uniforms, their heads were shaven clean and their old attires were burned down into ashes; and right after that, they were all shown their barracks, their bunks assigned and then ordered to go out and wait for new commands. Lieutenant Petrov wasn't lying about breaking them, as the physical training was too much, even for Rupert, who was used to work out regularly, maintaining his good physique. They had to drag their bodies around the mud loan, run several miles around the course, jump avoiding several obstacles and climbing walls. When the day was over, they all wash the dirt off in the communal shower and he lay down heavily over his sturdy and uncomfortable bed.

With all the training, he quickly drifted away dreaming on Grisha's embrace, his lips, his hands and his voice whispering how much he loves him.

Grisha arrived at Belinsky Manor defeated. Rupert's departing was a huge blow against his heart, and with the gentle music of a piano concert, he reminiscent of the loving moments with him. Time went by so fast and everything around Belinsky Manor screamed Rupert to him, but his walls fell as he grabbed some of Rupert's used shirts. The scents of his perfume hitting his face like a loving caress on his cheek, and he couldn't contain the tears anymore. He sobbed. He stood in the middle of the room, holding Rupert's shirt and crying silently. The butler saw him cry inconsolably from the slightly open door of the room, and lowering his face, he closed it behind him; letting him vent his tears alone and uninterrupted. After an hour of constant cry, no more tears came out him, so he walk to the bathroom and run a warm bath. Inside the tub, he remembered Rupert's smile as they swam in the warm beaches of the Bornean Island they stayed for a while. How Marci's disappearance faded in the past, and how slowly Rupert seemed to be pull towards him.

And as uneventful as their friendship came, their first kiss happened in one of their many walks by the beach on sunset. A slight gust of fresh air brushed against their sweaty skin and their lips fuse together as the stars appeared in the sky and the moon rose, casting white light against the sea. Waves went in covering their feet, breaking the tender kiss they share, and they both chuckled at each other's foolishness. He smiled making ripples and tiny waves in the contained water of the bathtub. And he sighed heavily. His heart melted in the hopes of getting his lover back.

So, as silent, as he was, he walked back to the room and crawl up in the bed. The same bed he had shared with his departed friend. His heart pounded strongly, trying to be brave for the lonely nights to come, and he curled in the bed sheets; still holding Rupert's shirt. His perfume made him feel close, and he didn't want to forget. He denied his senses to forget anything about Rupert, not his touch, his skin, his eyes, nor his smile. He closed his eyes and saviour Rupert's taste in his mouth; he listened to his voice in his head, his laugh and felt his hands holding him back.

● ● ● ● ●

In a spiralled rampage of uncertainty, Hans Voikevich walked constantly in his home, trying to figure out what to do now. He sold his own homeland for money, and eventually, everybody would know he was the mastermind behind the attack on Moscow and the imprisonment of many Russian citizens abroad.

"I've been trying to contact Mr. Braun for weeks and it has been impossible – it's urgent!" Voikevich told Eli Braun's assistant on the phone.

"I know sir, but as you know, our chief counsellor has been very busy…and…" she stopped suddenly. "He will answer your call now – please hold." She said with a strange change in her voice.

Minutes pass, and all could Hans listened on the phone was the soothing sound of an instrumental melody. Impatiently he stared at the streets from outside his private office in the city. He knew the Amerikans could track his calls; an even more dangerous to him, his calls could be tracked by the Ministry of Security.

"Hans!" the deep voice of Eli Braun jolted him in his place as he greeted him effusively. "I am so sorry it has been so long since we could talk. How are you, my man?"

"How am I? How do you think?" his voice reflected his discontent with everything. "I need to know when and how I will be picked up by the extraction crew."

"Yes – the thing about that – is that unfortunately, we don't have the crafts to infiltrate in your space without being detected by your ministry of security – If…" he said.

"If what?"

"If only you could somehow reach one of our camps around the surrounding countries."

There it sunk into his stomach; he could have made an agreement for money, security, and position if he sold out his own homeland, but the Amerikans weren't going to make things easy for him. The loneliness of his actions finally reached him and he swallows thick saliva, feeling the emptiness of his private office. Frantically he ran to his home and ordered his wife and servants to pack bags without telling anyone why they should. A phone call came in from the Hall of Ministers asking him to immediately go for the interrogation of Nikolai Isayev, former minister of tourism and national enlightment; and he couldn't believe the police actually caught the Beheader of Moscow, but what was more impressive was that someone so close to them, was a feared and ferocious criminal.

At the Supreme Court of the Ministry of Justice, the man called 'the Beheader of Moscow' sat in a small grey cell. The cell had no mirrors and no windows, just a hard bed with a thin mattress and a small toilet bowl, no toilet paper. Obviously, that cell wasn't used for longer periods of time. With his back against the wall, Nikolai Isayev sat, staring at the empty space before him, contemplating about his unknown future. The cell felt cold, but all he do was sit silently looking down and rubbing his hands slightly. The sliding bar doors opened and he turned his head towards the officer standing outside the cell in his black uniform. A peacemaker. Everyone was so afraid of what he could be capable of doing that they didn't dare to send a normal police officer to escort him. He stood up and was handcuff by the peacemaker. When he stepped out the cell and into the hallway, he saw the other three officers outside. They went through the hallways of the Supreme Court and as they meet people on their way, they immediately ran off from the sights of Nikolai, who was only walking with his head down in front of the four peacemakers.

In a round courtroom, fourteen ministers sat talking about the impending interrogation as Hans stepped in fixing his jacket and looking for his seat. Nikolai came to a halt at the entrance of the courtroom where his interrogation will take place and the four peacemakers stood behind him. He swallows saliva staring at the lustrous black floor. The anticipation of the upcoming interrogation was unnerving, and he could feel anxiety growing inside with every heartbeat. Detective Sawyer arrived at the courtroom with the minister of justice Ator Pozharsky with his powerful presence, by his side. All the ministers took their seats, right before Tsar Sebastyan and the Grand Duke Prince Aleksander entered the room, in their opulent and grandiose outfits; everybody stood up in their presence and waited for them to seat up behind the judge at their judging thrones, for everybody to see.

"Bring in the accused!" the judge ordered and the peacemakers pushed Nikolai on his shoulder to move. Peacemakers were trained to have no feelings towards prisoners, their sole job was to maintain order and follow commands.

With his head down, Nikolai walked towards the chair in the middle of the round courtroom under the eyes of all the ministers and the Royal head. Everybody sat silently staring at Nikolai, the infamous Beheader of Moscow, looking crestfallen. One of the peacemakers brought a tactile scanner and Nikolai was order to put his hand on it. Reluctantly, he thought it twice before lifting his right hand and putting it over the scanner. He felt the heat from the white light from the scanner, as it travelled up and down his palm detecting every detail of his fingerprints. An error came through the scanner and they all look at each other stunned, but the peacemaker was order to scan the hand again. Unfortunately, to the whole party, the scanner sent again another error and everyone contained their breath.

"That's impossible!" detective Sawyer gasped surprised. He stood up and walked towards Nikolai who kept his head lowered all the time; whose heart pounded harder and harder, and he could feel the slight trembling from his limbs. "Look at me!" he yelled to Nikolai. But he didn't look up. Violently, Vladimir Sawyer grabs his face from the chin and lift it up, to look directly at the face. Undoubtedly, it was Nikolai Isayev, but the fingerprint scanner wouldn't make a mistake twice for sure, and he wondered how was he doing so.

Strangely, the face of the man before him was of the same man he talked for long periods before; but still, it felt different, somehow all that time since that day in which he paid him a visit regarding Zatara Lukoskaia's whereabouts, has changed slightly his features.

"Speak!" he ordered furiously at Nikolai, who kept his eyes close. In a single instant, as the man in front of him opened his eyes and stares at him, he remembers the look on Nikolai's eyes, the fearlessness of his soul, the unapologetic personality, and the compassionate person he met when everything erupted in chaos. This man wasn't anything like that. This man was afraid of what was going on.

"Impossible" he muttered with his eyes open widely.

In this enormous world, how could it be that two persons over millions, share the same physical attributes? Vladimir Sawyer gave two steps back and his eyes watered with anger and confusion.

"What is it detective?" the judge asked perplexed with his behaviour.

"We need to identify this man." He said turning around and the judge lifted his right eyebrow finding ridiculous his petition.

"This man is Nikolai Isayev, the infamous Beheader of Moscow – He can't fool us – he does not need to be identified." The judge answered hoarsely.

"Your honour, this isn't Nikolai Isayev!"

"What? – How can that be? – Is that true?! – Who is he then?" everyone in the courtroom started mumbling.

"Order! – Order!" the judge called out.

Tsar Sebastyan stood up and everybody silenced.

"Could you prove what you are saying detective?" he said looking serious at him.

"I've been in the presence of Nikolai Isayev in countless occasions, and I can testify this man, as strange as it sounds – looks like him but is not him."

"You are the one trying to fool us! – We have been also with the accused, and we see him sitting there and we see Nikolai Isayev!"

Nikolai stared nervously at the whole thing. He knew things weren't going to be simple, but he never imagined they would reveal everything. *What's going to happen to me?* He asks himself as detective Sawyer asks a witness to identify him.

Katya walked in the courtroom trembling. She stood behind where Nikolai was seated, looking nervously at her surroundings; the ministers looked disconcerted at her presence there.

"Who's this?" the judge asks angrily.

"This is Katya Fedorova, she served the Isayev family for many years." He said announcing her. "There's nothing to worry about." Vladimir walked towards her, gently taking her by the arm. "We need you to identify this man. – Tell us if he really is your former master."

"But – I…" she stuttered terrified of confronting a dangerous criminal, even though she knew Nikolai for a long time.

"It's ok. He won't be able to hurt you." He tried to comfort her.

She swallowed a little saliva and took deep breathes before turning over to face Nikolai, who stayed silent the whole time. Her eyes became teary as she stares at the man sitting in front of her. If she would squint and doubt, she probably be fooled as everyone has been until then. But the slight differences in the physical features were enough for her to widen her eyes surprised with the resemblances. It was as if they were twins separated at birth, like mirrored images of each other with very little differences. An awkward smile grew in her face. It was outstanding.

"He is not."

The courtroom exploded with loud arguments, which quickly

diminished again by Tsar Sebastyan, as not even the judge could tame the animosity of the crowd.

"How can you be so sure, young lady?"

"I've worked for the Isayev family my whole life. I've seen master Nikolai every day since I was six years old. You could say we have grown together." She said trying to gather courage from inside her.

Vladimir Sawyer turned to the accused, grabbed him from his shirt lifting him slightly and getting very close to his face. "Who are you?" said with mad eyes.

"Detective!" the judge reprimanded his furious behaviour. "We will take a blood sample." He signals one of the peacemakers as detective Sawyer released the tight grip from his shirt.

With a pen-like device, the peacemaker took the blood sample from the accused's hand and the results were immediate. Trembling with fear, his eyes became watery lakes of desperation, his mouth open a little trying to catch his faltering breath as he sat staring at the judge and Tsar Sebastyan.

"You are not going to speak…" Detective Sawyer muttered, and the imposter turned his sight back at him. "How much did he pay you?"

"You are not just covering up a criminal – he is a traitor to our crown!" The judge directed his words at him.

The imposter looks around at the several peacemakers taking tight grips on their firearms and guns, at the tense look on the eyes of the ministers of state and in the disappointed look from the Royal Highnesses. He knew it wasn't worth, and yet he had no choice but to go as far as he can. There was nothing that will get him out of the mess he voluntarily got into.

● ● ● ● ●

"What will happen to that man?" I said as we sail back again after the inspection from the British navy of the Europa Empire.

"I don't really know…" Anichka looked away. "But he knew that he wasn't going to have a nice time."

"Why would a stranger give his life for me?" I asked confused.

"Ha!" she laughed. "Get over yourself…not everything is because of you…he had his reasons, you…" she stared back at me "you are just a medium for him to receive what he wanted."

I've always been an important person. I was surrounded by servants my whole life, even I thought this man was doing this all for me, that these men with Anichka were here because of the money I was giving them, and I was in command and everyone served me; when in fact, I was no one to these people. I was no one.

ELEVEN

Anatoliy stared at the sky through the leaves from the top of the trees, as he stands resting his body while doing his new job. His life is been filled with a series of horrendous tasks and he found solace in nature. In the movement of the leaves, the shapes formed in the spaces between them, and the serenity that was transmitted from looking away for just one second. The wind blew against his body, lifting the revolting smell from below and he lowers his sight to stare again at his important job. Mounts of decomposing corpses in a communal grave covered with quicklime stood at his feet. His job was to grab as many corpses as he could and dragged them to a crematorium nearby. That was the ultimate degradation for them. They could easily imagine staring at their own bodies been transported to the crematorium by some stranger. That's what the Amerikans wanted.

Every time they open the crematory, they could smell the flesh of the bodies they put in, and as they pile the ashes to clean the crematory, specks of dust covered their bodies as a greyish fog. They battled hard and struggled with the terrifying and dehumanizing job they were assigned. So looking back up at the sky, Anatoliy could dream of being away; being back at home, holding his children tightly and kissing his wife tenderly. He was a strong man, but circumstances had made him softer. His will was broken and now he was only a ghost of whom he used to be.

He couldn't stop but wonder how long would it take for him to be dust and ashes, as he stares at the ashes being washed off his body in the showers and going down the drains in a grey slushy stream. He covered the tears in his eyes with the pouring water from the faucet and cried for the uncertainty of Natasha and Sofy's well-being. He cried for his own weakness. He cried because he felt a failure to his own family, to his country. They all deserved better, they all depended on him and he failed them. His stomach turned, but he didn't have much food in it for him to be completely sick.

"I'm sorry…I'm sorry…I'm sorry." He cried repeatedly very faintly, hiding his pain from the rest of the prisoners of the camp. Not like anyone would judge him. They all have their own fears and their own pain.

An alarm went off and dogs began barking as he walked out the showers and some privates ran towards him pointing at him with their guns, ordering him to lay in the floor with his hands over his head. Scared he did as he is been told and his freshly washed body was once again soiled with dirt and he turned his head to one side to look at several soldiers running away with their flashlights on. *Someone is trying to escape*, he immediately thought. Minutes later he was pulled up by another soldier, he asked if he could at least clean himself in a nearby faucet but instead he was ignored and escorted back to the dormitories.

“You can sleep like that for tonight…Gryaznyy!” the soldier said pushing him on the shoulder. The Amerikans used simple words in Russian to denigrate more all of them. No one has ever called him filthy before he ended up under the Amerikan yoke. And as he ascended in the deteriorated steps of the stairs, several gunshots were heard making him jilt in the floor scared of them. The soldier kicks him and pulls him up, and more gunshots were heard. Trembling he walked towards his bunk bed and he lay staring at the bed above him, he didn’t notice the empty beds around him. He could listen to the soldiers walking outside, laughing and mocking the cries and pain of his fellow comrades; So he closed his eyes, as he knew he would have the infamous task of bringing the dead bodies to the crematorium or to the communal grave.

● ● ● ● ●

Natasha looked at the maid dress lying in the tiny bed, in the small room she was brought in. The house was as big as the house she used to govern back in Russia. White columns in a front porch, supporting the balcony in the second story of the house; delicate details of art, wood, and freshly cut flowers were set around the many rooms in the house. She couldn’t see much when the cadets brought her in, but for what she glanced off, it seemed it belonged to a highly ranked person, someone as rich as she is; or was. The tiny room was depressingly painted in a creamy camel colour, and a tiny desk with a lamp and a bed was all the furniture in it.

She walked towards the doubled doors in the wall and looked at the two other light blue uniforms hanging. Every step she has taken in this imprisonment has been a reminder of the many things she has lost. The silk, chiffon, taffeta, laces and fur dresses; the jewellery, the makeup, and the perfumes.

"Stupid woman, you can admire your room some other time!" The housekeeper burst in the room hastily. "Change into your uniform and come down to the kitchen." She said leaving her alone again.

She took off the raggedy clothes, put on a pair of underwear and slide the cotton dress over her body. And she sighed at the tender touch of the cloth against her skin. It felt like heaven in comparison to the rough and dirty clothes.

"Eva!...Eva!" A woman yelled while calling for someone, as Natasha walked in the kitchen.

An elegant woman walked in as she stands next to the housekeeper. "Eva, I've been calling for you like crazy!" the woman said looking annoyed.

"I am so sorry madam. I was getting the new girl ready." The housekeeper apologized for her imprudence.

"So this is the new one." The elegant woman said looking up and down on Natasha who stood silently covering her uneven short hair with a matching cloth of her uniform.

It was strange as everything in this new life for her, to be on the other side of the housekeeping. There she was, dressed in a maid's uniform in front of a rich and elegant woman; in high heels, impeccable dress suit, perfect and luscious black hair, tan skin and enviable jewelry. She felt like nothing, and the mistress of the house was not going to make her feel any more than what she was.

"I hope she is a quick learner." The woman said. "Eva, please tell the cook to make three cheese zucchini au gratin, maple glazed tuna fish and black sangria…I have the craving for something sweet and refreshing."

"Yes, madam. Is there anything else, I could do?"

"Give - this one the silverware." She said giving a smirk at the fragile Natasha. "What's your name?" she asked.

"Na…Nat…Natasha." She stuttered afraid of the woman.

"Natasha…" the woman muttered between her teeth and looking down on her. "I'm lady Giorgianna Samuels. I am the mistress of the house and you will address me as madam whenever you are told to do something."

"Yes…" she answered, "Madam." The words were hard to come out for her. She was once a maid, but not for very long. Somehow she felt it was harder now to get used to a life of hardships after tasting the joys of comfortable living.

"We will see if you are not as useless as the girl before…I like my silverware spotless." Giorgianna ordered as she walked out of the kitchen.

Eva conducted Natasha to the pantry room, where a table was set for when the silverware or any other task regarding the kitchen tools had to be performed. And there she sat in complete isolation, surrounded by drying herbs hanging from threads attached to the ceiling, jars filled with grains, boxes of fresh fruit and vegetables, and several cans of all kinds of food. She stared at every single thing for a while and her stomach grunted out of hunger. All this food around her was sweet torture and she didn't know if she would endure it without caving to the temptation.

With her shaking hands, she grabs a white cloth and takes a little silver polish as she starts her job in this strange home. With every stroke of her hand over each piece, her stomach grunts more, painfully whining for food, and she trembles a little trying to keep her composure. Breathing heavily she looks around after a couple of minutes polishing the silver cutlery. *I could just eat one tomato, perhaps an apple, or a fig*, she thought as her eyes wandered around the room picking up single items no one would notice. The noise outside in the kitchen wasn't distracting her. In fact, she knew they were all busy out there making the dinner the mistress asked for; and if lady Giorgianna was like how she used to be, she could be sure that none of them would stop until it was completely and perfectly done, afraid of their lady's fury.

Minutes went through, and the delicious scent from the meal prepared outside in the kitchen filled the pantry, making her hungrier than how she was already. Her mouth trembled, staring at the reachable and inaccessible food around her. She battled inside to grab anything, but the hunger from the malnourishment won, so she stood up and walked around and three boxes of strawberries caught her eye behind some blueberries. *Perhaps they have forgotten about them – I could eat one and no one would notice*, she thought while her fingers grabbed the perfectly ripped strawberries. Her mouth watered as she bites the strawberry and the juices began to flow out of it, and she sighed with relief as the fruit went down her empty stomach. And one after another, the strawberries disappeared from the box she grabbed from the shelf.

● ● ● ● ●

Grisha sat in the dining room in Belinsky Manor, while the butler Sergei brought in his breakfast and the mail. Silently he picked fresh cut fruit from a bowl and glanced at the pile of letters sitting next to him over the table. They were all letters for Rupert's parents but one; one was from Rupert himself directed to his parents, and with the letter in his hands he glanced outside through the window.

Grisha tightens his grip on the letter as he remembers the warm glow of the sunset, hitting his and Rupert's bodies as they stroll down the white sand beach in the improvised holiday they jumped to. It wasn't that long ago since the two were together, isolated from everyone;

completely free to share their feelings, to share his love for Rupert and finding solace in each other's embrace.

"We should tell our parents about us," Rupert said standing still abruptly and as Grisha walked a couple of steps forward.

"You think we should?" Grisha answered turning around and looking back at Rupert saddened at the thought of been rejected by anyone.

Being attracted to someone from the same sex wasn't something out of the ordinary, but people always stayed judgemental. Hiding was the right policy in situations like that, even if everybody knew about different relationships, but with no proof; it was similar to mistresses and affairs. Everybody knew but everyone kept silent, as long as relationships between same-sex members or love affairs didn't touch their lives. The world advanced in technology, time and rights; but few things remain the same, as people have been hypocrites since conception.

Rupert walked closer to him and gently caressed his shoulders with his bare hands. Their feet sunk in the sand and water hit their legs, cold in comparison to the heat of the sun. With his right hand, he lifts Grisha's chin and lovingly caressed his cheek and stared into his eyes for brief seconds.

"I don't care…I just…" he said with an affectionately smile, "I want you…I never thought I would feel like this for another man…but your soul makes me feel complete."

Grisha's eyes filled slightly with tears emotional at the words from his lover. "Then let's write them." He said. And as the sun sets in the distance, in the lonely beach, Rupert leaned in for a kiss; and they fused passionately, sighing for each other's taste.

He looks down at the letter as his reminiscence of Rupert's lips and opens it slowly.

"Dear Mother and Father,

The holiday has been a great idea for me to take. With all the things that happen, I felt guilty and now I am feeling less responsible for everything. Grisha has been a great friend. I don't know where I will be without him by my side. His support has given me the courage to confront my feelings and accept that there wasn't much I could have done to save Miss Weston from disappearing.

Since I was very young, I felt I had to be strong; I had to be the winner of every contest and the most mature of all of us. The fear of having lost control of a situation was too overwhelming for me. I knew Marci for very little time, and still, she was my gest, she was under my protection and I failed to her. I don't want to fail to anybody, not you...nor me.

I have found happiness on this holiday. These islands are a paradise on Earth, and I wouldn't imagine experiencing this magnificent place with anyone else but Grisha. With all my sincerity, I have realized how important has Grisha come to be for my mental health and me. At first, I was apprehensive on letting go any judgement; and I am sure you two will find it hard to understand and comprehend how something like this could happen. But I have never felt this way before. It's like my world has come to a settling point. Everything seems brighter, filled with hope and filled with happiness. If you could feel or sense the love warming up my chest as I write these words, you wouldn't doubt twice about the reality of this. Grisha has found a way to fill my heart with the joys of a unique kind of love. I don't see me without him; I can't imagine a life without him. I love him and I know you will understand.

Yours dearly,

Rupert"

A couple of tears started flowing from Grisha's eyes and he crushes the letter with his left hand.

"Sir, some of the workers want to speak to master Rupert," Sergei said walking in the dining room. "When will he come back?"

He brushed the tears away and trying to get his composure "master Rupert won't be back any time soon." He said rearranging his clothes.

"But what will happen with everything Sir?" confused the butler walked nearer.

"Don't worry, I'll be in charge," Grisha answered after a couple of seconds of consideration. "I will need to see the books of the house and tell the workers to come to the study."

"Yes, Sir!"

He sighs as the butler left the dining room and he glanced at the construction sites of the house.

With great remorse, he sat in the study listening to the complaints of the workers, as they have been none stop with the reconstruction of the house and they haven't been paid in weeks. He understood the upset feelings from all of them and as much as he wanted to please them and see that the reconstruction was finish, he couldn't afford the complete funding of something that big. So he chose to let the workers go with their workdays paid until further notice of continuing the construction.

"I believe it's the best decision." He said as the workers leave the study.

"I will have to ask for you and the rest of the servants to get a temporary leave as well," Grisha said while writing down a letter.

"How so Sir?"

"I won't be staying here, and I don't really know when master

Rupert or Lord Belinsky and lady Belinskova will return."

Sergei stared at him while sealing the letter and standing up arranging papers on the desk. "Most of us have no place to go Sir." He said.

Grisha glanced at him and saw the affliction on his face. That old man has spent his whole life in service to the Belinsky family, to some people who weren't his actual family, and now he was alone. They were all alone. He felt sorry for him and the rest of the servants. He walked towards him and grabbed him by the arm.

"You could stay here and look for the house." Grisha smiles compassionately. "But I can't guarantee your salary. I believe Lord Belinsky will be glad to know that you are taking good care of his property and there won't be any problems on compensating you."

TWELVE

Two housemaids carried silver trays with a ceramic tea set, macaroons, petit fours and cookies to the backyard of the Samuel's mansion, to the white gazebo in the middle of it, under a massive lavender wisteria tree. Natasha sets the table as the maids approached her, as she straightens the silk lace tablecloth and began setting the table with a big white centerpiece of white roses, a couple of the lavender wisteria flowers, green foliage and small white flowers.

Everything seemed similar to how she used to have tea. The pastel colours of the petit fours hypnotized her in her place.

"Olga you will stay here and serve the ladies. Alyanna and Natasha, you two will come with me…there are still a lot of things to do."

Natasha had to scrub the shower and bathroom, as the new girl, and every corner of the white-tiled room had to be spotlessly clean. Every step Natasha gave around the house was a reminder of how low she has fallen. With a damped cloth with a little cleaning detergent, she cleans up every golden faucet and detail from the bathroom. She cleans up the crystal bottles in the vanity and her hands look dry with flaky skin, from all the work she was enduring. Her long perfectly cut, clean and polished nails were gone, even though she had to be showered and deeply clean to work in that grandiose house, she felt as dirty as she belongs to trash. That is how she really felt, like a piece of trash.

She stood up and gave a quick glance at the beautiful gazebo in the back, where Giorgianna and her friends gathered to have some tea and desserts, chatting and gossiping. Sudden pain in her chest came and she took a tight grip on the cloth and the bucket's handle, clenching her jaw, clearly jealous of the mistress of the house.

"You think you are a smart girl, but he will forget about you, once he uses you." Krystina Isayeva's words came to her mind as a karmic ghost reminding her of her misfortunes. She was vicious to her and her mouth quiver thinking on that period of her life. All the lies she said, the schemes she concocted. Now they meant nothing. She won the battle against Krystina, but karma has finally reached her, making her pay for all the bad she has done in her life. Her reflection in the mirror caught her attention and she turned to look herself over it.

She thought on how the night before was so surreal for her. She was certainly not good at all before, but in very little time, she has fallen so low to stealing a box of strawberries and she enjoyed it. She would have felt better if she enjoyed stealing something of value, but a tiny box of strawberries has become so valuable to her, that she rejoices in the fact that no one caught her.

She took the bandana covering her shaved head and gently brushed the little hairs growing from her scalp. Her fingers travelled down her face as she studies her new self. Her heart beat faster with the anger and the impotence of her whole fate. Then she quickly turned around, disgusted with the sight of herself, walked out into the master bedroom, and stumped with Aiden, who was taking his jacket off and throwing it over the sofa next to his bed. His eyes opened, surprised at her presence and they glistened with the opportunity of having her alone.

"Sorry." She said lowering her head.

Right before she could leave he stopped her, blocking her way with his broad physique.

"I hope you are better here than in the factory." He said looking down at her, very close to her face.

"Ye…yes…" she muttered scared of his proximity.

"I am glad." He said as she looks up and his hand goes over her lips.

Nervously she trembles and excuses herself, leaving the room confused. *How was it possible for a man like him to be interested in a woman in her condition, mostly with the disgusting sight of her looks?* She knew she was far from the beauty she used to be; she knew she was a broken doll, and as she descends the spiral wooden stairs and she glanced back again at Giorgianna with her friends; that same spark that ignited with Krystina, awaken in her. She wasn't going to let an opportunity like this to go away; it could mean that she could go back to her old way of living.

"Natasha!" Miss Eva shouted at her, reprimanding her for her blatant misbehaviour, so she ran off as quickly as she could with her head low.

"Olga please tell the cook I want my berry and nuts mix."

"Yes madam!" she answered making a curtsy and leaving across the loan to the kitchen.

The kitchen burst in energy, with the cook and her assistant making dinner, when Olga walked in and asked for Giorgianna's order, while Natasha left the cloths and bucket in their places. The cook rolled her eyes, clearly annoyed by the order, as Giorgianna seems like an impulsive woman. She ordered Alyanna to help her look for the ingredients in the pantry. Natasha was given some shoes to clean and polish, so she sat in a nearby tiny room with a table and several house cleaning tools and started her assignment. It seemed like all she was ordered to do was polish this and polish that, and her hands were resenting the strenuous work they have been subject to and the strong chemicals. Her fingers started to become stained from the shoe dye and wax.

"Where the hell are the strawberries?!" the cook exclaimed angrily at Alyanna, so loud that Natasha could listen to her and the shoe she had on her hands dropped over the small table. Her senses falter, and she felt the ground at her feet wobbly as the cook and the girls outside discussed the disappearance of the box of strawberries.

"Mrs. Giorgianna is going to be furious." Miss Roberts, the cook said, "So if any of you took it better say it now…You all know how she is with her berry mix."

"We know, but none of us took it, Miss Roberts," Alyanna answered distraught while mixing the different kinds of nuts and berries in a white bowl with blue flowers and golden accents.

"I bet it was the new one…" another girl muttered upset for being accused of taking something she hasn't.

Natasha's heart stumped like an electric hammer, so strong she felt her chest bumping with every beat. Trying to keep her composure, she grabs the shoe with her hands and tries to continue polishing them, but her mind was unravelling different scenarios for her fall or punishment from Giorgianna.

"Either way if I don't take the mix to her, it will be worse for us," Olga said taking the bowl with her and exiting the kitchen, worried of what will happen next.

In the small tool room, Natasha could only imagine Giorgianna's reaction. She stepped out a couple of minutes later and everyone was working silently. Mrs. Eva sent her to water the plants around the house and to pick the dying flowers from the vases. Giorgianna seemed to be a woman who kept her house extremely tidy, and in that she could relate. The house felt lonely as she proceeds to do her job when she came back to the kitchen she found all the servants line up in front of Giorgianna, as she interrogates them about the missing box of strawberries.

"You all know how picky I am with certain things in the pantry, especially the ingredients for my berries and nuts mix…" she said pacing in front of them as Natasha slides herself in the group and receiving a stern look from her. "And it's not like I have prohibited anyone from taking something from the pantry, right Mrs. Roberts?" she asks looking at the cook.

"Yes, madam." The woman answered twisting her apron.

Everyone seemed nervous about the whole meeting.

"But when it comes down to the things that are scarce in the whole pantry until a new re-stock, I get pretty… annoyed…If I am not able to consume what's meant to be mine." She paused a little while looking at them. "And you may think I am overreacting for a tiny box of strawberries, but actually I'm upset for what that box represents."

"We are…" Alyanna tried to apologize but Giorgianna stopped her by only lifting her hand gently.

"I feel betrayed by all of you." She continued as she stands still in front. "I was embarrassed in front of very important women today. I looked like I can't manage my own house, and that's unacceptable!"

"What's this?!" Aiden walked in.

"Just a little meeting my darling. Nothing to worry about."

"About what?" he asked confused about the whole thing.

"Someone ate one of the three boxes of strawberries and I was…" he immediately shut her up.

"This is about a stupid box of strawberries."

"Well…I received lady Ford, lady Ashby, lady Howard, lady Massey, and lady Greenfalls…and how you think it made me look when I ask for something and I can't offer it to my guests?" she said trying to explain her motives for calling the staff's attention.

"I am sure those ladies will get over the lack of a few strawberries…" he said, "Everyone is dismissed, go back to work." Gesturing at the staff. "Mrs. Eva please serve dinner now."

"Right away Sir." She answered and gestures at the maids to get the silverware and start setting the table.

"Aiden!" she called him out in an indignant tone, "You can't dismiss them, I haven't finished."

"You have finished." He said turning around and grabbing her by her arm very strongly.

Natasha stared at everything that was happening in front of her scared that her identity as the strawberry thief might surface and scared of these two incredibly strong masters. She looked at the tight grip Aiden had on Giorgianna and it was a reminder of a similar scene between Anatoliy and Krystina. The same day she made her move and finally seduced a very faithful man, almost sealing Krystina's destiny.

Is this History repeating itself? She thought as Giorgianna and Aiden left the kitchen towards the dining room.

• • • • •

Curled up against the rocky wall of a damp cave covered in moss, Ivan Voronov and a couple of cadets try to keep their body heat up, as they could hear in the distance from the opening of the cave, a raging storm hitting the ground with fury. Their bodies tremble as the temperature goes lower and lower with every gust of wind that blows inside the tunnel they were in. With no hope of getting any warmer, they wait silently, feeling their wet clothes tight against their skin and listening to the eerie melody from several leaks around the cave.

Ivan clutched his hands feeling the ache in his bones, his broken skin, and nails. Water dripped from his hair, down to his shoulders and crossing down his back, making him aware of one piece of the rock pressed hard against one of the sides of his back. Someone shifted in his place, making the sound echoed in the place, and they all watched him. It wasn't fun to be trapped in a strange cave in a strange jungle, million miles away from home and cold.

A lightning stroke the heavens outside, partially lighting up the cave and they all glance around with their dirty faces while thunders growled like a pack of furious mythical beasts. Ivan scratched his stubble beard and nervously continued, as he asked for the rain to stop, so they could keep running away. The bleeding wound from one of the cadets wasn't looking good. The blood had almost turned black, and his uniform has fused with the crimson colour emanating from it.

More thunders growl in the distance, like a heavy reminder of the battle they endure and of how cowardly they runway towards the jungle to save their lives. The morale was low; the men were hungry and the memory of the screams of his comrades, filled Ivan's mind with desperation.

Trying to escape from all the interrogating eyes of his subalterns, Ivan steps out the cave into the opening and down the grass in the middle of the jungle. The rain seemed to be ending and chills travelled through his body as the wind blew against him.

"We have to do something for Frederik." One of his men approached from behind.

"I know." He said rubbing his hands, warming them up and stared up to the clearing sky above the treetops.

THIRTEEN

Three days later, we arrived at a foreign port. Anichka's men had everything prepared for the next step for our escape. With the fake Nikolai Isayev being judge and convicted in my name, things would probably be smoother now for us to go away. We hid in an abandoned warehouse and as I stepped in, I immediately knew it wasn't safe for Krysi to be in an environment like this. I wonder if it was a mistake. Rusty chains swung from the metal structure and dangled around the place. Puddles of water accumulated around the debris and patches of grass grow scattered on the broken cement ground.

"You know what to do," Anichka said while holding a small velvet clutch bag. She opened the small bag and handed two glass vials with some blood to one of her crewmates.

"Now we just have to wait." She said to me.

I couldn't imagine the reasons why we needed to wait. Still wait was what we have to do. This escape plan was filled with suffering waiting hours and having a baby with me wasn't fun. At least my little baby girl was a very calm child and wasn't actually giving me real trouble.

Somehow, the damped floor reminded me of Bea's underground dungeon laboratory. I could feel the chains from our victims rustling against the floor, and when I close my eyes and listened to the chains been hit by the wind, I could experience the fear they transmitted. I could salivate in expectation and my heartbeat thumped on my chest like a perfect rhythmical drum. In my mind, I could see myself walking around the dungeon, my hands resting against the cobbled wall and Krysi's weight similar to a severed head.

The door slamming brought me out of my trance and Anichka's man walk in. He handed her two digital tickets and waited for the final transaction.

"So I guess we have reached the parting point," I said as she walked towards me.

"You didn't expect for us to hold your hand all the way. Besides, once you reach the destination of this tickets, it's ought to you what will you do with your life." She smiled mocking my sudden nostalgia for the company in the journey.

Therefore, after she gave the instructions of my final escape, I was taken in a turquoise rusty vehicle to a precarious, old and broken down train station. I waited for the train with Krysi on my arms and my bags resting on the floor. The station was a lonely place, there was an old man smoking in an attending booth and a big rat ran in the distant corner. Dirt and dust accumulated around the place and I didn't even think once it has been the first time in my life that I have not been in impeccable places since I chose this path. The path I am actually escaping from, this path that jeopardizes Krysi's future and her wellbeing.

I stared at the shrubbery on the other side of the track resembling the tall hedges of Rozanov Manor. Everything I've done has been endangering for my own self, but still, I feel like something is missing. I've lost so many things. I have lost my family, my mother, my revenge on Natasha, my love for Josephine, and my life. Suddenly the rails started screeching as the antique train approaches with the noisy motor and its rusted locomotive. This wasn't a high tech or advance vehicle as it was in a tiny town in the middle of nowhere, and probably few people use it, yet it was going to be a great vehicle for my enterprise. It was low key and with the poor technology, we would be able to go through towns quickly. A metal sign on the top of the station swung as the locomotive pushed to stop right in front of us. The white worn letters of the sign gave me an immediate hint of where I was, and unsurprised I sighed. Anichka and her crew left me somewhere in Germany. In a broken German I directed myself to the ticket collector/inspector and gave him the two digital tickets with our information and our destiny. The middle-aged man look at us uninterested, biting a toothpick between his yellow teeth, he checked the tickets and let us board the passenger's wagon. He, later on, walked towards the ticket booth and exchange a couple of words with the old man and gave a signal to the conductor.

The low and dirty aspects of the places I have been forced to go through in order to get away no longer astound me. Certainly, I am not looking forward to giving this kind of life to Krysi. Inside the wagon, only one woman sat with her head wrapped in a beautifully printed scarf in red. I sat a couple of sits away, trying to pass through the moldy smell that instantly hit me in the face when we got in. It was as if people travelled with farm animals on this train. The sits that looked like have seen better days, had all been covered in vandalized graffiti from past passengers and some of them didn't even had cushions or backs. I felt my stomach turn when I saw Krysi picking at one of the many holes in our black leather seat. Instinctively I grabbed her hands and distracted her with something else.

And it hit me.

I can't have her with me. I've been blind, thinking I am going to be able to give her the life she deserves away from all the madness, but selfishly or stupidly more like it, I have dragged her to a dead end. *What would become of her if I continue with all of this?*

The train was already on its way to the next station, and I couldn't escape this reality, I couldn't escape my reality.

● ● ● ● ●

Vladimir Sawyer sat silently in his office while staring at the ceiling. Peacemakers follow orders, they were like a militarized police force, and Tsar Sebastyan was a strict ruler. He has heard of the atrocities the peacemakers were capable of when the necessary force was needed to extract information from prisoners, but he has never been in an actual extraction. Fragments of the brutal extraction of information came to his mind as he tries to figure out why someone would go through the troubles of covering for a serial killer. Still, after savaging that man's body and almost leaving him as a living corpse, they got nothing out of him, nothing worth knowing. In fact, he remembers how truthful the look on the man's eyes seems.

"They are ready for the execution sir." An officer burst in uninvited.

"Ok." He sighed taking his jacket and putting it on as he steps outside the office.

In the middle of the Hall of Ministers, a steel post was set up and people began to gather around behind a barricade of peacemakers.

A wooden replica of the royal throne sat on top of the stairs of the Hall and nineteen chairs were set on the steps below the throne as Vladimir walked near the plaza.

“We can´t let something like this go public.”

“But if we don’t do something people will start to question our effectiveness.”

“Nonsense! that man is innocent!”

The minister’s debate linger inside Vladimir’s mind as he saw how they all descended to their seats followed by Tsar Sebastyan trying to look dominating.

“He is far from innocent.” Tsar Sebastyan said, “He chose to help a criminal escape. He may have not committed the crimes himself. Consequently harbouring the whereabouts of a highly dangerous criminal makes him as equally guilty as if he was the one carrying the weapon. The horrific murders and disappearances have stopped, and as far as for the civilians knowledge, we have in our hands the infamous Beheader of Moscow. I believe that as long as we don’t have more crimes of this savage nature, we can rest assure that the public wouldn’t mind if this man is, in fact, the actual criminal.”

They all stared at each other at the cruel and cold judgement the Tsar was making.

Vladimir couldn’t believe it. The people he worked for, the people he has sworn to serve have given their back to the law in order to save their positions and ranks above the common public. The unwritten laws of rulers weren’t something he personally signed himself for in the force.

The beaten man was carried out handcuffed and sadistically strapped at the steel post with his hands above his head and his feet tight to each other. The man’s breathing faltered and he clearly was battling to catch as much air as he could. The bloody wounds from his body terrify the crowd that look in awe at the grotesque spectacle.

"Let's pray for the soul of this man."

"We can't just let a dangerous criminal roam our country freely," Vladimir said interrupting the discussion between the Tsar and the ministers.

"We have bigger problems than one single 'criminal' walking freely detective." Tsar Sebastyan stepped forward looking down on Vladimir as if lecturing him. "If we don't solve our international problem with the Amerikan's, the Asian Nations or the empire of Europa there might not be a Russian Empire to rule and serve."

Vladimir stared silently.

"There are more people in danger if we don't solve that, than wasting our time with one murderer that actually hasn't committed any other murder."

"So all we are going to do is appease the masses? Give them what they want?"

"Detective, we are giving them peace in wartime."

"That's not enough. I enrolled in the police force to give justice and incarcerate the criminals; the bad seeds of our society." He answered displeased with Tsar Sebastyan's verdict on the matter.

"Are you defying his royal highness decision?" one minister asked upset with his sudden insubordination.

"I do!" Vladimir answered loud enough for everyone to hear.

"Think carefully detective – you've done a good job on this case." Anatole Globenko said grabbing him by the arm, almost pleading him to retract from his words.

"I can't continue serving a corrupted legislature." He liberated his arm. "I resign my position in the police."

They all walked to their seats and waited for the execution to begin. A strange sound came from the post and the fake Nikolai cuffed to it began to whimper and plead for forgiveness. His grunts roam like thunders in the plaza and his painful screams were highly pitch on everyone, as the post began to slowly elongate in several segments stretching his body to the max.

Women cry for mercy, some men applaud the sentence, and others felt the whole thing revolting. Vladimir turn around as the skin from the man began to tear up and blood started to run slowly from them. The screams and cries were loud, so loud he could still listen to them from afar as if he was still in the middle of the crowd. He turned around to see the man's flesh and bones showing from the separations and his body still responding by twitching slightly. Vladimir covered his mouth. The whole thing was barbaric. However, the man was already dead.

Hans Voikevich's heart rose more and more as he watches the man being stretched to his death in front of the eyes of the whole forum of ministers, his royal highness Tsar Sebastyan and all the pedestrians at the plaza, imagining being executed in similar fashion after everybody finds out how he sold his own country for his own benefit. He returned home after the execution was over. His wife Jocasta saw the whole thing from home and disgusted for the scene, she indulges herself with sweets trying to keep her mind from the horrors of the splattering blood, the tearing flesh, and the exposed bones. Hans stormed in ordering his servants to pack him a small suitcase as quick as they could. Confused, Jocasta questioned him for the absurd requests, as she knew there wasn't any plan for a trip, and in the madness of the afternoon he rose his voice to her ordering her to shut her mouth and to stop complaining about something she wasn't supposed to know about, lifting his hand almost about to hit her. Scared, she sat surprised at the rage from her husband, a rage she knew he had but he never tried to show it in front of the servants. Her maid stared silently trying to keep her eyes down as she waits to help Hans pack his things. Angrily, he walks away to his studio where he has a saving vault with money and jewels, leaving the two women alone in the bedroom.

The maid said nothing, as nothing she says would make things better for her lady, but all she did was give her comfort by grabbing her hand in complete silence. Jocasta smiled awkwardly, hiding the fear and keeping herself poised from the abrupt behaviour. The young maid was gentle with her, as gentle as a long companion in the lonely life she started having when she wed Hans. He was a good husband, a decent man and still at the same time he was heartless and dominant.

When everything was packed he left the house without telling anyone where would he go, leaving Jocasta standing alone at the base of the main stairs of the house and surrounded by the maids still carrying clothes and shoes in their hands. He got in his car and drove away; not too fast, not too slow; just the right amount of speed to not raise suspicions from anyone. He went through town and glanced over the plaza as he went by the Hall of Ministers, looking at the cleaners scrapping the rock-tiled floor of the plaza stained with the blood and flesh from the execution.

"That won't be me." He muttered as his car drove him away from the town towards an uncertain future. He could have taken Jocasta with him, but he had to think carefully about the consequences of being associated with him if the truth ever came out.

Natasha never felt the need to pray ever in her life, but for how things had changed, she felt nothing but the need to seek a higher power to intercede for her well-being. She needed as much help as she needs now, with all the crazy madness with the lost strawberry box and the unknown heights of Giorgianna's rage.

After a restless night filled with nightmares of the tortures she has suffered and the possibilities of more coming from Giorgianna, Natasha started her new daily chores with saggy eyes with deep dark circles under them. Holding a bucket and a cloth, the tedious chore of cleaning every glass window with her nude hands. The strenuous work she has been submitted to was bigger than what she ever experienced during her life as a maid back in her beloved Russia.

The house seemed strangely silent. Aiden left the house and Giorgianna sat calmly in the studio practicing her calligraphy. Olga brought her in some tea and annoyingly stood in a far corner after serving it.

"What is it?" Giorgianna asks after sensing her irritating presence behind her, without taking her eyes away from the paper.

"I am sorry Mrs. Giorgianna..." she approached her with fear and catching her breath. "I wanted to come forward about the missing strawberry box."

Giorgianna lifts her head up and slowly turns around to face her. Olga swallows saliva nervously and feeling awkward for her look. An ink drop fell over the paper making a splatter on her perfectly polished calligraphy practice. The black ink was absorbed on the paper slowly, while Giorgianna's mind settles on what Olga said.

"Was it you?" her voice almost quiver in rage.

"No...God no...Madam... I would never!" she said preoccupied. "I just thought that with how things happened with Mr. Samuels, you deserved to know the suspicions I have about the culprit."

"You thought wisely."

"Thank you, Madam."

"So who do you think it was?"

"That new girl...Natasha...you gave her the order to polish the silverware and she stayed for a long time in the pantry."

"Ugghh...that means nothing." Giorgianna rolled her eyes.

"I know Mrs, but she was the only one who had the time to actually snatch it and we all know those are your favourite strawberries and are off limits...and...well, she's recently arrived and she is probably hungry."

Giorgianna sighed looking around, pondering on the slight coincidence of Natasha's arrival and the missing box. "Olga, thank you for your honesty. I will figure out what to do."

"I am at your service...I just don't want any of the other members of the staff to know that I was the one who told you."

"You got nothing to worry, now go back to work."

She turned around back to her calligraphy practice as Olga walks away from the studio. When she was finally alone in the room, she looked down on the paper, her hands crumple the practice paper and she pursed her lips. All the possible things she could do to Natasha travelled around her wicked mind. Mostly for the humiliation, she endured in front of all the service staff. She will definitely make Natasha pay for everything and with her dainty hands; she shrivelled the practice and throw it away in the trash.

● ● ● ● ●

Ivan looked around at the damped cave and his fellow demoralized cadets. The last food ration they had was a day ago and the fresh water they were having come from the intense rain that pours down in the jungle. Frederik look pale and weaker with every hour they spent there and he knew he had to take a decision sooner or later. Standing at the entrance of the cave looking outside at the greenery from the jungle, listening to the insects and the strange silence of the whole.

"We've got to do something about Frederik. He is not looking well, Sir." Leo said.

"We got no choice but to surrender," Ivan said sighing with regret.

Leo only stared saddened with the feeling of failure. They escaped from the mouth of the dragon and they will walk back to it with their tails between their legs. Ivan walked back into the cave to break down the bad news to the rest of the weaker soldiers. He knew when he was first to deploy to the Pacific, that things so far away from home would certainly be hard, but he never envisioned part of his path to be so rocky and hard to deal with. Surrendering wasn't an option for a royal army member, and it broke his spirit to face his cadets and tell them the wrenching decision he had to take.

Inside the cave, the men look demoralized, rubbing their skeletal faces and achy muscles for the comfortability of the rocky surface. They trained hard and tough to overcome many things, but never to the extent of risking their lives deliberately.

"Luck hasn't been on our side for quite some time…" Ivan started figuring out the correct words to say, but truly, he knew nothing was going to be right about what he needed to tell them. "You all know Frederik's health isn't getting any better and if we don't do something soon we might lose him."

The men glanced at each other in the gloomy cave.

"I've decided to surrender." He went direct to the point like an arrow thrown at a bullseye.

"We can't!" someone yelled.

"Yes, Sir! I agree with 'one eye' we've come far and survived this long to simply surrender to the enemy."

Ivan walked around them with difficulty, trying to avoid the rock on the cave's ceiling. He kneeled next to Frederik and gently put his left hand on his shoulder. Frederik lay tired, asleep in the rocky damped floor. His chest moves up and down with struggle, and Ivan sighed at the thought of the death grasping a member of his crew under his command. Many had perished, but this couple of men had been with him since they escaped from the maws of the Amerikans. He felt responsible for the fate of these men, young men who have been giving their lives to protect the crown and the royal family.

Josephine" he sighed again asking her beloved wife for some type of sign on what to do. A green butterfly flew in the cave, in the middle of all of them; in the middle of the sadness and stillness, she graciously lays on Ivan's shoulder and as quick as she flew in, she left. There was the sign he was asking for. Josephine was with him all the time and no decision he makes would be wrong as long as he believes is the right one.

"I am not asking for any of you to come. I am not going to tell any of you to surrender." He said glancing up at the scattered and weary men. "Frederik needs medical help; I don't know if we are going to get it…But I have to try…I will surrender for him to get better."

His eyes shone with loyalty and bravery, but the men weren't completely impressed. Right then, he realized how much the war has changed every single one of them. The war that was still raging on outside the cave, somewhere.

"SS…Sir…" Frederik reached to Ivan with great struggle, his wounds seem to be worse. "Please…don't…" battled to say in his languid state.

"The decision is made dying here isn't an option for you." And after a couple of minutes, and as Ivan finishes on gathering some of the scattered belongings, the rest of the crew make the decision to accompany them despite the degrading thought of surrendering.

In his almost catatonic state, Frederik could feel the warmth of the sun hitting his face gently and jumping shadows from the trees above them, as he is being carried to the nearest Amerikan military base. The tall grass of the jungle was tough to walk through, and in every single one of their minds, they remember how hard it was for them to run away, how Frederik got his wounds on his back from those infamous Amerikan drones. If the Amerikan's had developed such horrible weapons, only their imagination could travel far enough, to believe what horrors might the Asian countries had researched and advanced.

The screeching sound of the several claw-like tendrils that spout the drones and the painful scream of his comrade as the tiny nails scratched his back tearing clothes, skin, and flesh apart.

The Russian armoury was one of his kind long time ago, and somehow, even though men keep enlisting to the forces and the country kept its stand as a major adversary if a war wavers; the country fell in feeling comfortable in its position, while outside, the world kept changing and the countries and kingdoms kept evolving. It was sad to experience first-hand the horrors of the safe place Russia has been since the peace treaty.

They could have been walking hours, and he knows for sure they made several rests on their cavalry back to the devil's moat.

Ivan chokes when they devise the base in the horizon. He knew they must have been watching them from afar, or with a drone because they wouldn't have been able to get this far if they didn't want them to. As they each gave a step forward to their new fate, drones flew over them and station in mid-air pointing tiny green lights from their weapon's socket. Armed men ran towards them in every direction, circling them and enclosing them in a small space, and Frederik coughed, spitting blood from the strenuous travel. Then as unexpected as Frederik's cough, a slam in the back of Ivan's head leaves him unconscious.

Minutes were seconds, and hours were days. Ivan didn't know how much time has passed since they went in surrendering, and he was unconsciously placed in a containment cell and stripped down naked. His lips felt flaky and his mouth was dry, so he realizes it must have gone by a couple of hours since he ever drank any sort of fluid. His joints ached as if all the vigorous escape and the long surrender walk back was taking its final toll. The floor felt dirty, full of dust and the walls felt cold to the touch. His eyes gaze around the small space trying to figure out a way out, some crack from where he could look outside and he tried to listen in the silence for any sound. What had happened to his men? To Frederik?

He leaned his head against the wall, closed his hand in a fist and held it against his chest imploring to the almighty God for some hope as he tries to control his breath and his jaw anxiously trembles.

● ● ● ● ●

Grisha rested, while the long-distance train took him away to his family summerhouse in Italy. The transcontinental speed train was one of the fastest transportation vehicles in the empire. It was one of the many trains, which connected every continent and every city to each other. With the almost collapse of the entire civilization with the drone war, borders were open to every citizen in the world and the series of underground tunnels and above ground tracks were a complete and peaceful collaboration of the entire world. Little those pioneers in the peace knew about the events that would make countries, kingdoms, and continents to close back their borders and making most of the tracks inoperable. Only a few open-borders remained open for use in the whole system, and the one that conducted to Italy was one of those. The change of scenery was soothing to the conflicted mind of the poor Grisha. He was tired of everything. When he finally thought happiness was knocking at his door, the new impending war between worldwide forces brought him back down to the loneliness he suffered for so long; not feeling he fitted completely in society. The comfortable seat embraced his body as a cradle and the view from outside the window calms his feelings with its tender beauty. Luscious trees, blooming flower pastures and a couple of sporadic houses every now and then, tried to keep his mind off from

Rupert's fate.

"My beloved Rupert,

My heart has succumbed in great sadness since your enlisting..."

He wrote a letter to Rupert before leaving Belinski Manor. With every word, his mind wandered in the remembrance of Rupert's smile, his laugh, the twinkle in the corner of his eyes whenever he was being cheeky.

"I am leaving Belinski Manor to my family's residence in Italy, as I am not able to stay there without you as everything reminds me of you; and besides, I can't afford a grand estate like it as you didn't leave me in charge of any income to sustain it. You have a very loyal staff, and they are willing to stay there until your return. Oh Rupert, wish you didn't enlist. Wish you were with me. Wish...I wish nothing had ever happened, and yet I am so grateful because, without all those events, I wouldn't have connected with your soul the way I have. I will write to you every week until your return. I thought I could write to you every day, but it wasn't going to do any good for us. I know you miss me too as much as I miss you; but I respect your decision, and I know it is something you have to do; so I am giving you, your space and time to focus on your search."

As he leaves the letter at the army post, his last words hit his mind like a spear.

"Please come back safe to me. I don't really think I would be able to go any for ward without you. I'll keep you in my prayers.

With all my Love,

G"

Grisha wipes a slight tear that surfaced in the corner of his left eye, while an old man reading a paper glanced at him as he does that. A few passengers were scattered around the wagon and all their faces fell in the shadows as the train went in through one of the underground tunnels of the system. Flashes of small blue and bright lights came in through the glass windows, and slowly the inner wagon-lit itself with a dim yellowish light.

A screen lit up in front of him and a menu appeared in it. Time for dinner and he wasn't really hungry. The separation from his love has played havoc with the schedule of his bodily needs.

While eating the crab cakes and asparagus he ordered, he set the news channel on the screen. All passengers were distracted with their own stuff, some watching ancient films, others talking to their relatives, and Grisha sat there alone eating his dinner and watching the news. Why watch the news in the time like this? He wondered as most of the news was about the war and the political battle taking part in it. Then, the execution scenes of the Beheader of Moscow came through and his fork fell on his porcelain plate, making a loud noise but not loud enough for the other passengers to stare at him. The scenes were gruesome, and his heart beat faster knowing that man was once his best friend. Then the news anchor began to mention the names of Beatrice and Josephine, counting them as his last victims, and Grisha couldn't believe that Nikolai would harm his precious Josephine.

Not because he was sure that his once friend, wouldn't be able to harm anybody, but because he devoted himself to Josephine, and he idolized her so much that it was sickening to look at. The world has turned darker, and no one's life would ever be the same; but even though Nikolai must have suffered greatly with the execution, a sigh of relief escaped from him, like the fact that the authorities had put an end to the killing spree he was on. *Why would someone do things he did?* He asked himself rubbing his right hand across his face, wanting to understand, but not being able to.

● ● ● ● ●

"Anything good on your letter?" Charlie, his once servant, asks Rupert while folding his clothes over his bed.

"Not really…" he sighed. "But given the circumstances of the situation we are living, nothing is good and nothing is bad at the same time."

"Newbies! Time to train!"

Again, another training day after the other. It seems like all they do is learn meaningless self-defense and the mechanisms of weaponry. After a long day, right before going to sleep, their captain speaks to them about what will happen.

"The Ministry of Security and Armed forces have decided that you would graduate tomorrow."

"What?" someone gasped surprised.

"You will all be assigned to pre-existing units and will be deployed in several places of interests for our crown. If you all follow your orders, we might stand a chance to conquer this milestone in our contemporary history. Now rest, because tomorrow you will need all your energy."

The captain left the barracks and the lights came off. The slight tint of the light from the moon gazed through the windows as they all try to wrap their minds around the news.

"Why would they send us to battle if we have barely trained?" Charlie said looking up at the worn out and dirty ceiling.

"They probably need more men abroad…" Rupert answered. "This is not a common small battle between countries, the whole world is at the turmoil and we are the centre of discord."

"Why can't we just go back to the peaceful life we had?"

"I doubt we will ever get that back. It's part of human nature to take control, to seek power and wealth."

"But you are a wealthy oligarch yourself." Another cadet spite as their conversation was open to anyone.

"True…But if you knew what I have been through and the things I didn't realize about the ones around me, you wouldn't doubt that something in all of that would have changed something in me."

"You are just talking bullshit in riddles."

"Hey! If he were just another rich man, he wouldn't be risking his life alongside with us." Charlie refused.

Rupert stared at the top bed. The crusty bedsheets, the uncomfortable mattress. He has traded his amazing life voluntarily for this. The barracks were cold, and he seeks warmth under the thin sheets. Somehow, with all the lack of commodities, he felt he was doing something right with his life. His life now had a purpose more than getting money, social climbing or pursuing pleasure. Sure, he was separated from the one person he is fond of as he has never been, from the owner of his heart, from the only one who has seen him for whom he truly is; but still he knew he had him, he knew that when he comes back, they would be happy; he knew things would be better. It could have started in a bumpy road and with a sudden separation, but it could end in an eternity of happiness and love. Morpheus played his music and he slowly drowses off with Grisha's eyes batting his eyelashes and his lips saying how much he loves him.

FIFTEEN

As if things weren't rough enough for Natasha in the foreign lands, Giorgianna was making her life even miserable, complaining about her lack of skills on cleaning, polishing, and upkeep of a house, making her do twice and thrice the same chore in one day. Certainly, she knew she wasn't in good graces with Giorgianna, but she never expected the sudden change towards the worse, as in Giorgianna's sight she was nobody. Sometimes she swore she noticed how the other maids, smirked and giggle at the way she was being treated, but even though a burning desire to stand up for herself grew inside her, she couldn't risk the little things she already has. At one moment of the day, her luck shone right back again, while she carried a tray with tea and biscuits to Lieutenant Samuels and in her heart, she hoped she could get the chance to be alone with him.

Aiden sat in his desk reading some reports on the soon strategic incursions and course of action to defeat the Russian empire, while Natasha walked in with the wooden tray on her hands almost shaking in anticipation; looking for courage in her heart to speak up. She left the tray with the tea set on a serving table and began serving his cup, giving slight glances at him. His stern look was menacing. After serving, she stood quietly and nervously playing with her fingers.

"What is it?" he asks upset with her presence.

"uhm…may I have a word, sir?" she managed to plead in a broken voice.

He looked up at her and after his eyes travelled up and down her shaking body, he nodded and offered her a sit with his right hand while adjusting himself in his leather chair.

"I…" she started with her hands clawing down on the wooden arms. "I am very grateful for what you did bringing me here." A knot in her throat made it hard for her to express her train of thought.

"There's nothing to be thankful for." He smiled. "Since I first saw you, I found a special interest in you."

Natasha blushed.

"I know I am in no position to ask for something, mostly after your generous behaviour towards me. But you see, sir…I have a daughter…" she lowered her eyes as they start to show some tears in their corners. "She was taken from me, and I want to know where she is and if she is fine." She looked up directly at his eyes trying to get some sympathy from him.

He stared at her considering her petition. He stood up and walked towards her slowly and calmly. She felt his eyes burning over her shoulders as he comes to a stop next to her and she could sense the heat from his body. Nervously she looked down on to her skirt and back up at his eyes. He was so tall and broad. Silently he pushed another chair next to her and sat leaning forward and grabbing her cold bony hands.

"I will help you find your daughter. I am sure I can figure out where she was taken." He said with certain warmth beneath the coldness of his eyes.

Her face lit up and her lips tremble not knowing completely how to react and what to say; she actually didn't think it would work at all talking to him.

"Thank you sir!" she answered containing her tears. "I don't know how I can repay your kindness."

An awkward silence followed and his right hand reached towards her face and caressed down her cheekbones, making her shivered at his gentle touch.

"I am sure we will find a way."

Suddenly his smile and inside warmth were not as kind as she thought it was. Cold lighting went through her spine making her shiver slightly. It seems like all she could do was behave naively of his intentions and advances, even if she felt defenseless under the claws and eyes of her predator.

● ● ● ● ●

I looked down on the Italian picturesque street. I have managed to get a small flat and settle with Krysi after our escape. Italy is so much different from my beloved Russia, the terracotta and brownish colours of the stones, the colourful blooming flowers on clay pots, the laughs, and giggles from neighbours and the white linens flipping in the air as they dry under the bright sun.

"Beautiful," I muttered admiring it all. Coming here was the best decision I made for Krysi's future.

A knock on the door and I answered worried at whom it might be. I am still not used for outsourced house cleaner service and as my new maid walks in and starts tiding up, I finished getting Krysi ready. I looked at my moneybag and I have known for days already that money won't last for long.

"Mrs. Nervetti, do you know if there are any job offers around the town?" I asked the old woman while she grabs the used bedsheets and stares at me a little confused trying to translate in her head all the words I said. "Lavoro...Sto cercando..." I scramble the words in my mind wanting to be comprehended by the woman. If I'm going to stay here I need to learn to practice more the language, which I knew already but I'm rusted in it out of lack of practice.

"Lavoro per un gentiluomo come te?" she shook her head thinking what kind of job a man like me could do. It was obvious that I wasn't skilled at many practical things, yet she didn't know my management background and my great skills with a knife in my former murdering strike.

"I don't mind il lavoro...I need to fornire per mia figlia."

"Ci sono alcuni negozi giù città in cerca di aiuto, forse si potrebbe trovare qualcosa." She said hunching her shoulders.

"Centro?"

"Centro!" she said waving her hand in the air. I didn't quite understood much about what she said, but I figured out she must have said something about jobs downtown. I had no real choices than to go down there and look at every shop and business until I find something.

I went in and out of shops and small businesses looking for a job. The language barrier had been proven to be a major factor for me not being able to find something, and once I was to call it quits for the day, I saw a butcher's shop from across the street from a small café I was just in.

"What else I got to lose?" I muttered looking down on Krysi in my arms.

Bells chimed when I pushed open the door of the butcher's shop and the distinctive smell of raw meat and blood punched me in the face. I panted and my eyes shut with the memories of old hunting, the screams of the hunted, the tenderness of the flesh in between my fingers; and I swallowed saliva pushing through all the past joys of my former life, to be focused in the present.

A young woman came out from the back with a warm smile. "Come posso aiutarti?" she asked standing behind the glass counter filled with different cuts of meat and beef.

"Uhm…" I look for the words in my head.

"Buongiorno Giovanna! Come stai oggi?" the bells from the door chimed again and a woman walked in with a basket full of food.

"Buongiorno signora Albano. Si prega di dare un'occhiata in giro. Mentre io frequento questo giovane gentiluomo." She said and turned back to me waiting for an indication or reason why was I there.

"Prima attend la signora," I said stepping back and letting the woman sort herself out.

After a couple of minutes and when the woman was gone I tried again to find the right words.

"Io non parlare molto italiano. Io looking for lavoro." I said in broken Italian.

"I knew you were…straniero…foreigner." She said. I felt relieved somehow someone else could communicate with me without any difficulty. "I will ask mio papa, he is the owner." She turned around and left me with Krysi alone in the middle of the shop.

Mr. Caporale was a bulky man in his fifties. He and his daughter Giovanna took charge of the butchery when his wife passed away two years before, and the fact that I was a single father trying to make a living was a major factor for that giant man of Mr. Caporale to agree of my employment.

● ● ● ● ●

Beaten. Broken.

Ivan dragged his scrawny being alongside other prisoners as they walked in the concentration camp. The phantasmagoric scene was one of many Anatolyi had seen many times since he was brought in by the Amerikans. The brutality of the war was the common bread eaten every day, and with every fellow compatriot being brought in, it was as if the Great Russian Empire wasn't as great at all. Ivan's soulless eyes looked around at the rotting wood barracks, the mud his feet sank with every step and the broken faces of other Russian citizens. For him, it was a double defeat. His eyes watered at the state of most of the war prisoners. *Why was his life spared?* A knot built up in his throat remembering how foolishly he thought on believing in the hospitality from the enemy by surrendering and getting medical attention to his crewmate.

Soldiers pushed them and dragged them towards their new homes. Cattle. Dogs. Animals. Nothing more than a thing under the eyes of the Amerikan military. Powerless, everyone had to look silently at the unfair misbehavior or look away. After being assigned their places and left as sacks in the obscurity and dampness of the barracks, Ivan stepped out to muddy patio of the camp, and somehow in the middle of despair, sadness, hunger, and sorrows, little children play around oblivious to the realities of the actual danger they have been living in. And his eyes watered. He failed to his crown, to his people, to everyone around him. He felt shamed and humiliated, and couldn't dare to look at the faces of the people he has failed to liberate.

"Ivan?" Anatoliy asked approaching him from his right side.

Ivan lifts up his face and looking at a familiar face, even if it was a tired, broken and dry out the sight of what they used to be, made him fall into pieces and a few tears rolled down his cheeks. His chest contorted in pain and his breath faltered, as Anatoliy embraced him in his arms as if he was his father. Anatoliy was the first face from his former past that he sees in months, and even though it was someone outside his family it was comforting to know he wasn't alone in that rotten place.

"What happened to you?" Anatoliy asked looking down on him confused for his strange brokenness.

In between the arms of his old friend's father, Ivan recalls the horrors of the tortures he endured, looking at the dirty and gnawed clothes they both wore. How he was strapped down a metallic chair, geodes attached to his naked body and a machine transmitting high charges of electricity through him. His sphincters loosen up and his bladder relieved itself; and his excretions ran down his legs, under the laughs and mockeries of his torturers. He swallowed saliva trying to forget, but with every minute passing the images kept coming one by one. The searing pain as the electric conductor was pushed in through his urethra like a catheter, making him passed out for seconds until the high electric charge shoot right through him, waking him up.

"Nothing," Ivan muttered.

Anatoliy didn't believe him. His body showed signs of brutal torture.

"I am glad you are fine." He said to the poor young man.

"Inmate 3007!" a soldier yelled calling for Anatoliy. The deep hoarse voice from the soldier made Ivan shudder and hunched himself shaking, wanting to pass unsighted. The tattoo numbers burned his skin as he saw his friend walked away towards the soldier after being called. It was strange to see a young man, once strong and brave, shivering and hiding as if that person had completely disappeared.

In another exhausting workday, Anatoliy carries bodies from one pile to another and to the incinerator. In between the piles of deceased a strange tattoo in the arms of the bodies caught his attention. The hammer and sickle ink art, was as fresh as it was done a couple of days ago, but a closer look at the body demonstrates the looks of a man in his thirties, and they had those symbols tattooed early in their admission to the army. Only ongoing members and former members of the royal army had that symbol tattooed in different places of the bodies.

Sudden sadness hit his soul. The man must have endured a lot of pain as wounds in his back had a disgusting black and greenish tint to them. Coagulated blood poured out like clogs when he and another prisoner lifted the body. A knot formed in his throat. He has seen a lot while being imprisoned, but still, his gag reflex reacted when something revolting happened in front of his eyes. As they turn around to pick another body, the same tattoo appeared in the arm of the new body. Then something struck down his mind. He hasn't actually seen any military men from the royal army imprisoned, and somehow these men belonged to the army.

"Help me hid them." He asks his workmate, who looked back at him strange by the request. They left the bodies behind some bags of clay and continue with their macabre job.

Staring at scrawny children play around in the dry mud by the scorcher sun, Ivan lingered between the dead and the living, dehydrated and hungry; his hands tremble in the stone like stillness he was.

As a failure, he saw the day go by unmoved. No one cared to help him or feed him; it all meant too much work and less food for everyone, and for the soldiers if he died it only meant one less dirty Russian roaming around in the world. So once Anatoliy and his workmates came back, covered in the ashes of the bodies they incinerated in the day, he was still sitting in the same spot with his sight lost in the vast emptiness of the horizon.

It was depressing for everyone to be in captivity and for the soldiers it was entertaining. Sometimes at nights, when the soldiers were drunk and having a jolly time, they made some of the young boys dress in skirts to dance with and have some other men play musical instruments for them; and they laughed and spit and broke a little more the poor souls. The ones that could sleep at night, only dare to have nightmares as their dreams have turned sour, the others, simply spent restless nights fighting the terrors, the hunger and the ache from their bodies.

As the sun rises and their miserable lives continue, Ivan stares at the top bed of his. He wondered how those wood bars kept the bed above him together without breaking down on to his fragile body. A cold and rough hand grabbed his arm startling him all of a sudden.

"I need you to come with me today." Anatoliy leaned in. "I am going to ask for help and I will ask for you."

"Why?" he asks sitting on the uncomfortable bed.

"I think there is something you need to see…Maybe you will be able to help us escape." Anatoliy confessed, frowning his forehead with painful hopes.

Anatoliy left him and he looks around at the other men dispersed, scratching their dry and flaky skin, their bald heads; while some just had their head lowered, some covered their faces, maybe sobbing and others stare at anything in the barrack.

When the truck arrived to pick Anatoliy and the other men for their workday, Anatoliy came forward, and awkwardly asked for help as one of the other men had sprint their ankle. The man leaped showing a clear wounded ankle, and under the unpleasant complaints of the Amerikan soldier, he suggested telling Ivan to come with them, pointing at him as he stands at the steps of one of the barracks. Gesturing with his head, the soldier calls upon Ivan, who awkwardly follows the orders.

Ivan's uneasiness grew as they reached the workplace. The stench of rotting corpses brushed against their faces making his stomach turn and the soldiers laughed at him, kicking him to go on to work.

The soldiers left and Anatoliy asked him to go help him pick up some clay too. As soon as Ivan's eyes looked down onto the hidden bodies below the bag of clays, his heart began to pound harder and faster, as anxiety hit his body as a flush of heat all over.

"We found these men yesterday and I thought I should show them to you…to know what you make out of the fact they are here," Anatoliy said looking back and forth from the bodies and Ivan.

"I…no…I can't!" Ivan rushed away.

His sight was jumpy from tree to bush, to rocks, to ground and his body. His breathing was agitated and faltered at his erratic behavior. He stops at a tree leaning against its raw bark trying to focus his blurry sight. Anatoliy followed him confused and worried from afar.

"Ivan…are you ok?" he asked posing his right hand on Ivan's shoulder.

"Don't!" instinctively jolted at the proximity. He turned around, looking with his teary eyes at the branches of the trees above and surrounding them, the brightness of the sky and pressing his back at the tree, he slowly sat down on the ground, covering his face and moving his head from side to side.

"Those bodies…I can't…" he sniffs. "The blood…they…I shouldn't…" he suddenly looks away.

"You are making no sense."

A brief moment of silent went by, in which the wind blew moving leaves and branches.

"Their blood is in my hands."

"No, that can't be! The presence of those men and you here mean our army is working to save us."

Another silence.

"I don't know…I don't want to put your hopes down, but we are not here because we were trying to help, not because we had no will to help, but we had to surrender…and things happened…"

Anatoliy looks back at the pile of bodies and the other prisoners.

"I should have saved them. It's all my fault." Tears ran down Ivan's face. "If the Tsar is fighting to save us, is beyond my reach…but we are trapped here…we can't do anything."

It was obvious that Ivan's spirit was broken down, but it wasn't until that moment in the middle of that strange land, that no real hopes should be harbored.

● ● ● ● ●

"Florence…here we are again." Grisha sighed as he steps out of the train at his arrival in Italy. The station seemed solitary, as most people are scared of the world war boiling slowly and the tensions growing between nations. The tap of his shoes echoed through the emptiness of the building. An old lady sweeps some dust from the floor and she looks up at him with a serious face. Stepping outside on to the road, no public transport vehicles near, so he stood there waiting; watching cars go past the station, not crowded with traffic but it was certainly quieter.

Finally, he saw a taxi and was on his way to his family mansion. Secluded from the outside world by an untamed wall of trees and shrubberies. He asked the driver to leave him at the front gate and he gently pushed the iron doors open. A cold wind blew from the left, making the leaves and branches hit each other as he walks up the path to the mansion. He sighs, as he can't keep his mind off from the memory of Rupert fooling around with him while they were abroad trying to forget Marci's disappearance. As the wall of trees became clearer and clearer, and he reaches the top of the hill, the brightness of the sky pushed through the top branches and the thick clusters of leaves; and there it was, Krupnov Manor, with the cold grey stone, and provincial jars with dry out flowers, dust filled windows and a certain amount of moss climbing on the walls. Ghostly, yet intact.

Dust flies off in the air as he pulls open the heavy drapes of a couple of windows to let the sunlight in. It wasn't that extremely dusted but the mansion needed some cleaning. In the bedroom, he stares for a while at the bed. The bedsheets were exactly in the same position he and Rupert left them. In every fold and crevice, every mount of fabric, the evidence of their love for each other. For a while he stood there, just remembering the gentle touch of Rupert's hand, his kisses, and his eyes as he looked down on him while they let their passions loose, how his hair fell over his forehead, his smile.

A knot formed in his throat and his nose became runny, as sadness filled his heart as he could remember how their hands separated the last time they saw each other; that last look into his eyes, that last moment of bliss. He walks towards the tall windows and looks down upon the horizon. The tiny houses in the village near, and the vast green lands surrounding the manor.

"I'll wait for you." He exhaled blurring the glass in front of him.

● ● ● ● ●

The faces of the people he betrayed, surrounded him as he crosses several towns on his search of an Amerikan base at the outskirts. The further he goes, in a deeper mess and nightmare he goes in unaware.

"I don't know where he is!" Jocasta cried upset, as officials interrogate her in her home.

"You are his wife…you are telling me you know nothing? - He is a traitor. He has given sensitive information about our bases and incursions abroad, risking thousands of civilian's lives."

"Look, officer, I am a disgraced woman. My husband left me; I wouldn't choose to be an undesirable member of society so easily. So if you ever find my husband, tell him I prefer to become a widower than have him back." She said with a strong stance and a serious face.

In the middle of the night and at a desolated road, Hans Voikevich came to a sudden stop as his vehicle was intersected by a troop of Amerikan men. He took a tight grip on the wheel and his gloves complaint at it. The men step out of their vehicles, their boots crushing the gravel and their non-friendly faces were slightly intimidating. Hans swallowed saliva worried yet hopeful they would help him reach Eli Braun finally, and escape from any danger from the empire. A couple of men stayed behind talking and started smoking, still giving glances at him inside his vehicle while one of them walked towards him securely.

"This is a far off place for a respectable gentleman." The man said leaning on the door of his vehicle and looking down on him, studying his clothes and the appearance of the interior of the vehicle.

Hans doubted himself timidly for a second before speaking up, "I am looking for asylum – officer…Sir – My name is Hans Voikevich and I'm friends with Chief Counselor Mr. Eli Braun."

The man stared at him. "Really?" he leaned closer under then base of the window. "And why our Chief Counselor left his friend ask for asylum on a lonely road in the middle of nowhere?" rising his right eyebrow.

"Well, …he told me to look for the closest base to where I was…I" He shifted in his seat, his body almost trembling completely. "I packed my things as fast as I could and…I just drove away."

"You see…" the man looked away towards his mates talking and fooling away where they stayed waiting. "Your story could be the truth. I admit." He bit his lower lip. "But I am not in a position to grant asylum to any foreigner that comes around this monitored area."

"Sir, I am an important member of the Hall of Ministers of the Soviet Empire. I am the second minister of foreign affairs in charge. I am just not any civilian!"

"To me you are a nobody, and unfortunately for you…I'm the law here…" he said and looked back at his men giving them a signal to approach them.

"I demand to speak with Mr. Braun!" Hans said desperately and shifting his eyesight from the approaching men and the man next to his window.

It was all a quick swift of time, and before he could do anything, the men pulled him out of the vehicle and cuffed him, to then push him violently to the ground and as his old knees hit the road, one of them hit him on the back of his neck, leaving him unconscious on the ground.

Nightmares became a reality to every Russian civilian under the regime of the Amerikan's while the war was waging abroad. But despite the fact that she wanted to wrap her mind around the idea that maybe, just maybe her life wasn't that bad, the strong perfume emanating from Aiden's skin embedded in her, the squeaking sound of the old mattress and the weight of his body pushing against hers haunted her new life. Aiden was a handsome man, but he was also a savage, a brute that prays onto her until he had his claws deep in her soul. Natasha couldn't do much but stare away from her undesired lover from time to time, as he forces himself in her, and think of the old days, the grand houses, the jewelry, the beauty and happiness of her former life. And in the middle of her torturous encounter, as he constantly ravages her body, Sofy appears in her mind, and a beacon of hope reaches her heart. And the pain was endurable. Her body served as a sacrifice in order to find her precious daughter and maybe a new life.

In the darkness of the corners of the small room, she could see standing the ghost of her sins in the forms of Krystina Isayeva, smiling at her pain and suffering. She whimpers at his thrusts and moans at his kisses, trying to convince him she was enjoying the encounter, but the fear deep beneath her eyes could only be noticed by her and her victim.

"Serves you well." The entity approached down on to them.

Aiden was oblivious to its presence.

"You are the whore you always were…" Krystina's ghost says smiling and looking down on her. She cries dry. "You won't have her back….You took her from me…and life has taken her from you."

Aiden lays on the bed, making her get on top of him and as he reaches the end of his pleasure he arches his back and Natasha moans hiding her disgust by closing her eyes, and she feels the hands of the Krystina's ghost pulling her head back from her short hair.

"I'll see you in hell bitch!" Krystina says as she exposes Natasha's neck giving the appearance of extreme pleasure.

As soon as everything was over, he stood up, got dressed while Natasha lay with her eyes wide and teary. "Do you know anything about my daughter?" she asks as she lays still under the bed sheets, her hands tight to her chest trying to cover her bare body.

Aiden sighs with discontent. "I do know where she is…" he starts to button up his shirt. "She is at the Institute of Wellness, a reform school for rebellious children we have in the city."

"Is there any way I can contact her?" she looked up with hopeful eyes at him.

"No – that's a lost cause." He sentenced picking his jacket from the floor. "Once a child is admitted in that place, their brains are lobotomized and their former memories wipe out." He glanced at her with an evil twinkle in his eyes "she is no longer yours."

Anger rushed up to her body and in a quick sprint she was clawing at Aiden's body like a mad woman, calling him horrible names for his deceit, he promised her he would help her and all he did was used her like a piece of paper. She was no match for an old man yet military trained soldier, and as a small pillow, he threw her back on the bed forcefully.

"You promised…You promised…" she muttered continually as he steps out of the room.

"Be ready the next time I want to make you mine again." He said before leaving the broken Natasha on the bed, her breasts exposed carelessly, and her eyes filled with tears and a slight sob came through her mouth. There was no fixed schedule for his visits. She washed, got into her uniform and went back to work; at least this time she didn't have to suffer his appetite while on duty, which usually consists of him forcing her in any room she was cleaning and forcing himself with no regard of her complaints. She seemed to had signed a contract with the devil when she agreed to his demands.

● ● ● ● ●

The warmth from the Italian sun was nice as it hits the face of the Russian troops while they are deployed in allied territories. Rupert reminiscences the countless summers spent with his beloved Grisha and Nikolai while still being friends and the odd fact that Nikolai became this strange and dark specter that took innocent people's lives.

"You left anyone back home? Any cute girl?" Charlie asked Rupert as they set the provisional tents on the field.

Rupert looks at him and grinned, "Not really." But in his heart, he felt the joys of knowing Grisha was safely back home.

"Well, I am sure you will meet someone special when we go back."

"Sure."

The camp was set in a couple of hours and as they step out of their tents to stretch their legs and look around at the place. Rupert could recognize the area, they weren't far from Krupnov Manor, Florence and the town buildings could be devised in the horizon also.

"This is the first time I am in Italy. How crazy is that?" Charlie said having a drink of water and standing next to him. Suddenly an aircraft flew over their heads grunting like a mythical beast and they stare at it as it goes away. They knew it wasn't one of their aircraft and the war was every second more real.

"Is there any girl back at home waiting for you?" Rupert asks still gazing upon the blue sky.

"Yes…her name is Katherinna…" sadness came through Charlie's breaking voice when he mentioned her name.

"We'll have to do our best to go back then." Rupert looks at him expressionless but determined in his words.

Their commander gathered them all around the middle of the campsite and explained to them how far they were from the nearest town, and the reasons they were settling there. The war was hitting more allied countries and was advancing more and more directly towards home.

SEVENTEEN

Atonement came finally. That day, things started ordinarily normal for me. Krysi was being a good girl staying in the nursery I found for her and arrived at the butchery early. Giovanna received me with a warm smile on her face and her father was already filing the knives. The tenderness and coldness of the meat between my hands felt soothing. And with every slice and chop from the bloody parts, I felt as my ability with sharp objects had finally a purpose.

I stare at my reflection on the glass of the showcase. My brown eyes glistened again. And my scrawny look was starting to disappear. *Would anybody recognize me, if I ever look the same as the old Nikolai Isayev? As the old rich boy, who danced and mingle at lavish parties, gobble on champagne and delighted with exotic foods? As the same terrifying demon, they named the beheader of Moscow?*

Through the main glass windows and doors, I could see Giovanna swiping the floor outside, in her yellow skirt with white polka dots and her white blouse and a flowery apron around her waist. Her dark hair swooping from side to side, up in a ponytail, and my mind wandered as I dreamt of having some sort of luck with her. She stopped, sensing my sight on her, as I stare looking like a fool, and waved at me with a little chuckle in her gestures. She reminded me of Josephine. My dearest love. If only we had something like this. If only we found a way to go far from our families, our duties, our shame, and our fears. We could have been happy. Beatrice's aftertaste came to mind. She is another victim of my reckless life. Of the sickness in my head. Suddenly customers came in, and my mind was occupied for a while. I could lose myself watching the mothers coming in with their children, the funny stories of the ones who needed someone to talk to and the various flirtatious looks from single women and girls who found the young butcher apprentice handsome.

If they knew the dangers of someone like me. Bad thoughts started to generate slowly from my unconscious. Like if for some reason something in me was asking to take somebody else's life. My body trembled with the thought of slicing, again and again, the warmth of the blood sipping through my fingers and the last breathes of every victim. I push those thoughts away. I needed to focus on Krysi, on the new life I have to ensure for her, on her happiness.

"Did you heard about the soldiers camping not far from here?" One of Giovanna's friends told her as they have a cup of coffee.

"I heard something but I don't like wars." She said.

"I don't like wars either, but I wouldn't mind a uniformed fellow courting me."

The girls laughed. And I keep my ears up as I cut a few pieces of meat giving them my back. Soldiers meant trouble for me.

The bell at the front door rang. A new customer. I grabbed a cloth and cleaned my hands. Nothing would have prepared me for the customer. Grisha stood in front of me stunned.

"Nikolai?" he called me out loud.

"Sorry?" My breath left my mouth completely and I pretended I didn't understand what he said.

"I thought you were dead!"

"I don't know what you are talking about sir. Would you like to buy anything?"

He stepped towards the showcase. If it weren't for the glass barrier filled with dead animal meat and pieces, he would have been really close to me.

"You don't fool me!"

"Sir, is everything ok?" Giovanna asks approaching him from the side, distracting him from me.

"That man is a murderer! You can't be around him!"

"You are confused Sir…my name is not Nikolai," I said trying to throw him off, but his eyes told me he wasn't buying anything I said.

"Sir, if you are not going to buy anything, I will have to ask you to leave." Mr. Capporale said from behind me as he came out of the back surprised by the commotion.

Grisha looks around confused and disturbed. His eyes watered and he gave a few steps back until he left the butchery.

"That was something!" Giovanna looks at me and I just shrugged.

That night I felt someone following me, but I didn't turn around. He is preying on me now, and for the first time in a long time, I felt the other side of the hunt. He wasn't giving up until he realizes I wasn't Nikolai, because so far for him, I looked exactly the same; even though Nikolai was months dead.

But penance comes in many forms, and for me, things weren't going to be simple or easy. Bombs were dropped at certain parts of the town, and as we crouched under the tables covering ourselves from what seems like an earthquake; my mind reached upon the destruction of the war in my beloved city. How broken and destroyed it left the grandiosity of majestic Manors like the Ovsky's, the charred trees alongside the road to Isayev House, the cries and desperation of the poor citizens on the streets. The happiness I found in rebuilding Jo's home, her life and mine.

Windows shatter as bullets were shot in all directions. Giovanna screamed in fear and as surprising as everything started it suddenly stopped. Then silence followed. Mist of dust covered the shop and the town itself. Giovanna was too scared to walk out, yet she reached her father and hugged him deeply.

"I have to go and look for my daughter!" I said, and they both nodded.

The town was broken. Debris from buildings scattered around. And still, I felt the worse must have been somewhere nearer because even though things look rough, it felt it was actually safe; giving me some hope that perhaps my baby girl was going to be fine. I jumped in between broken concrete and see people crying and cursing at the enemy. I saw boys and girls calling for their parents and my heart sunk with the idea of my girl being trapped or in danger, alone or even worse…dead.

I sighed with relief when I reached the nursery and Marina was there holding Krysi in her arms trying comfort her, while other kids were sitting around waiting for their parents. I walked towards them and held my girl in my arms. I cried my eyes out of happiness as I see her safe and well, and wondered what I have done in my life to deserve so much luck.

It was all chaos. And looking at my girl's eyes I knew I couldn't be as cold as I used to be. I felt sorry for Grisha and had to look for him, I had to see that he was ok too. Attacks and wars are terrible, and yet in moments of desperation, they are cathartic to the right soul.

Krupnov Manor wasn't far away. And as I search for a way to reach the mansion a group of soldiers in an armed vehicle were leaving the town towards the same direction of Krupnov Manor.

I stood in front of the vehicle to be noticed with my girl in arms, and they stopped abruptly. One of the men came out yelling at me and I tried to explain myself until they agreed to take me at least near the mansion.

● ● ● ● ●

Rupert looks around at the town near their campsite. Concrete walls and shattered windows were a constant note in the houses all around. The vibrant colors from flowers in the clay pots dimmed by the lingering dust in the air after the attack. He passes through butchery and saw a young girl trying to clean the front of the shop while a huge man, much older than her was looking at the shattered windows and pointing up, probably deciding with her what to do with them.

It was tragic. And sudden despair rushed into his heart like a stinging arrow, making him hunch a little and his eyes tear. Once you link your heart and soul to somebody, everything seems to affect your thoughts and even though he knew Grisha must be safe back home, he needed to be sure.

"We have orders to stay put. Another group will replace us later" Charlie said approaching him from behind catching up to his pace.

"Ok." He sighed

"Is everything alright?" asked frowning.

"Yeah, I just…." He sighed again, "Need to check on a friend's summer house. Just to be sure everything is fine."

"It's your friend supposed to be there?"

"No, it's just the house."

"Just a house?" Charlie snorted, confused at the request.

"It's important to me, alright?... He is a very close friend of my family."

"Ok, we can figure out a way to get there after our shift is done." He said waving his hands in the air. "But you will ow me a big one pal!" he said patting Rupert on his back as they kept walking around the town.

EIGHTEEN

Clarity is always at reach, even in the darkest of nights. We all come to a point of our lives in which we have to decide what's right and what's wrong. We made unconscious decisions every single day, and somehow we want a superior being to explain to us the whys and the reasons for the consequences of our decisions.

It's never easy. Never simple. And yet, with every decision we make, right or wrong, whichever it might be; we grow and learn and experience everything for a better outcome in our future.

Natasha sat silently in her room, once again unfulfilled and unsatisfied by giving her body to be used and abused, in order to recuperate Sofy. Her eyes tear a little and her nose began to run, as she sobs in her silence the consequences of her decisions; of her life. Sofy was never meant to be hers. She could sense the ghost of Krystina mocking her from the beyond as she didn't completely get what she was looking for.

She looks up at the ceiling. The cream paint from the ceiling she has been watching over and over, as Aiden ravaged her body constantly. She has tried to wash off his scent from her body, but her skin seemed to be impregnated with the wrenched and musk of his aroma.

She stands up and walks towards a small mirror in the room. Her hair has grown a lot more like a short pixie and even though once she would have thought that length was cute, her life was a complete miserable mess.

On another site of the country, Anatoliy, Ivan and the rest of the prisoners were kept outside their barracks for no explanation. The heat was strong as the sun hits their heads and burns their fair skins. Soldiers stood around them with guns on their hands and guard dogs next to them barking furiously at them. Suddenly, they were being separated into groups.

"What you think is happening?" Anatoliy asks as him and Ivan and other men are conducted to one side.

Ivan didn't answer back. He lacked will for living. In a zombie-like state he stood there and followed the lead he was given. That brave man and soldier were long gone by the horrors of the tortures he had to endure.

The scorching sun was starting to be painful on their bodies and the sweat was beginning to run down their backs and foreheads.

Anatoliy saddened at the remembrance of the crowded balls with delicious and extravagant meals; with rivers of booze, champagne and wine. The happy faces of his friends and family, the young folk flirting with each other. The joy of falling in love for the first time. He blinks pleading to god, the soon end of the war and their return back home with his children and wife.

Ivan's eyes wandered from soldier to soldier, trying to find an explanation of the strange behavior. He could be a shadow of a man now, but he feared the worse from this Amerikan men. He swallows saliva trying to keep himself awake and alert in his numb state. But the tortures he suffered had broken down his soul to his very core, making it impossible for him to control his fears. The ground and gravel felt hard on their worn soles. This was some kind of new torture, he thought.

"Is our country really going to do it?" Elle says, visibly moved, to Spencer on the phone while she watches Claudia play around with some dolls.

"It's not like it wasn't conceived in our plans." He says remorseless.

She brushes Claudia's hair with her right hand. Even to someone as heartless and tough when it comes to the foreign prisoners on the camps, she felt some sort of regret on the situation. But that's how life works. Conscience gives us the chance to retaliate if ever we choose the wrong decision; but if we decide not to, we would then end up having to deal with the consequences of our inactions.

In his studio, Tsar Sebastyan sat in his desk with his hands on his face covering his mouth as he thinks carefully about what he was just told, while across the room, the Tsarevna sat drinking tea and reading an antique book like nothing was going on in the world. Almost oblivious to the reality of her compatriots across the globe.

"Is anything wrong?" she says sensing his sight on her and slightly lifts her head.

"Of course, dear..." he says. " But...nothing for you to worry about."

In Florence, it was hard for Nikolai to be standing in front of Grisha with Krysi on his arms and Grisha's stern look down on him.

Took him a long walk from the main road up to Krupnov Manor, and even though he knew the reception wasn't going to be warmth, it was something he had to do.

"So it's really you," Grisha says hoarsely and upset.

Nikolai nodded.

Then a few seconds of silence weighed on between them.

"I want to make sure you were fine after what just happened at the town."

"Why?" Grisha snorted.

"We were once very good friends."

"So?" answered back immediately not caring for Nikolai's sudden guilt.

"For old time's sake." Nikolai's voice brakes a little. "I could have lost Krysi…" says looking down on her, who clenched tightly onto his coat, with teary eyes. "She is everything I've got. Everything I have done since Jo's dead…Agghh…" pain and suffering came through and finally he broke down, hunching over and hugging Krysi tight to his chest. "I loved her so much…I made a mistake…I could have saved her if….if only I didn't trust…"

Grisha looked at him ramble.

"Beatrice went mad…I should have known…she…she…But – but I avenged her…" he smiled wickedly, which suddenly turned into an uncontrollable and strange laugh.

"I can't do this anymore…" He looked up at Grisha. His life had taken a toll on his mental health and he would never be able to give Krysi what she deserves. A happy life. Because he was already tainted and rotten from his past evil doings. He puts Krysi on the floor and kisses her forehead. It was heart-wrenching and ultimately heartbreaking to make that decision. "Take care of her."

"What?!" Grisha bellow confused. But before he could pronounce any word Nikolai gave a few steps back and walk away.

Krysi's cry haunted his cowardly escape, but in his heart, he knew that was the right thing to do for her and her future.

"I wonder if he is fine." Anichka blurted out as she and her crew waited for any new job at a bar, looking up at the wood-paneled ceiling and the bright lights from the lamps.

"Who?" someone asked.

"Just someone." She answered, but she was clearly wondering about Nikolai and his daughter.

As soldiers conducted every group to their showers, cramping them all inside, including Ivan's and Anatoliy's group of men, Elle picks Claudia and puts her on her lap; Natasha stares angrily at her reflection and as she smashes the mirror, Tsar Sebastyan stands and looks outside the tall window of his studio sighing heavily. Giovanna helps her father swipe the shattered glass and concrete around the butchery, Rupert reaches Krupnov Manor and realizes his beloved is standing there with a young girl in his arms, right outside the main steps of the entrance. Nikolai reaches a river and stares at the flowing water run down the stream strongly. Blood drips on one of the sides of Natasha's, and she picks one of the big shattered mirror pieces from the floor, as her hand begins to cover completely with blood running down her arm as she lifts it with evil intent.

Screams of pain erupted inside the showers when the hot water began pouring out with jet-like strength against the beaten bodies of the men including Anatoliy and Ivan, whom with the same reaction as everybody rush towards the doors pushing against each other trying to find an escape of the boiling torrents, but it was inevitable. Soldiers laughed at the terrified faces of the prisoners still standing outside waiting for their turn with the deadly shower, as the foggy mist of the hot water been poured cooking them alive.

Natasha's eyes filled with tears, while she lays on her bed, falling into the hands of the angel of death, as her slit wrists pour her crimson blood out drenching the bed. She never thought she would have gone this way, alone in a tiny room, as a servant.

At Krupnov Manor, Rupert couldn't believe the story Grisha told him, but the more he looked at Krysi, the story seemed unimportant. He hugged them both. Krysi was still sobbing, and yet even at her tender age, it was as if she knew she was safe with these men.

"We will take care of her, right? she is innocent." Grisha asked him worried.

Rupert looks right into Grisha's eyes. He meant the whole world to him.

"I love you." He said forgetting Charlie was there too.

"I love you too." Grisha smiled and leaned in to kiss him. There was no need for a direct answer to his question. He already knew inside the answer.

NINETEEN

Nikolai looks back at the forest behind him. Peaceful it stood in the middle of a warzone. So much beauty. So much calm. He took his clothes off and turned back again to face the water before him. The twinkling reflections of light were mesmerizing and he could imagine just then what a happy and joyful life his little girl will live.

He smiles, takes a deep breath as the sense of relieving fills his whole body. He gives a step forward into the river and the water felt cold while the irregularities of the river rocks were slightly painful on his feet. He closes his eyes, listening to the wind, the leaves on the trees clapping as thousands of hands at his atonement. He let himself go, and the cold water engulfed his whole body. While floating in the silence of the currents he opened his eyes and stared at the blurry images at the surface. Slowly his mind begins to fade off and wander in the tranquility and alienating feeling of the waters.

Nothing outstanding happens. The world continues to revolve.

People continue to live, fight and battle in nonsensical wars; babies are born not even knowing the truths of the world they are coming to, and people of all heights of society and age die indistinctly. *Does my life mean nothing?* He thought as his consciousness vanishes into oblivion. Krysi's giggle resonated in his memories. Perhaps he did not do much good in his life. Perhaps he was not someone extraordinary. Yet, that tiny life he helped create represented a giant sun of significance to his life. Making it all worth living again.

THE END

ABOUT THE AUTHOR

Gerardo Canova was born and raised in Panama City, Panama. He grew up mixing his passion for well written novels with his inherit interests for science fiction, mystery, crime, suspense, and the paranormal. His debut novel 'The Twisted Life of Nikolai Isayev' received incredible reviews from the judges of the 24th Annual Writer's Digest Self-Published Book Awards, calling it a good book for readers who want to escape into a unique setting -- 24th century Imperial Russia -- and experience life through the protagonist's eyes. A world of wealth and violence awaits those who enjoy a fast-paced, intriguing story.

This is the sequel to that debut novel, and second book to be published while working on several other potential books in English as well as in Spanish.

www.ingramcontent.com/pod-product-compliance
Lightning Source LLC
Chambersburg PA
CBHW030814310726
48980CB00006B/495/J

* 9 7 8 9 9 6 2 1 3 2 1 8 9 *